Chip Hilton Sports Series
#9

Freshman Quarterback

Coach Clair Bee
Updated by Randall and Cynthia Bee Farley
Foreword by Dean E. Smith

BROADMAN
& HOLMAN
PUBLISHERS

Nashville, Tennessee

0-8054-1991-8

Published by Broadman & Holman Publishers,
Nashville, Tennessee
Page Design: Anderson Thomas Design, Nashville
Typesetting: PerfecType, Nashville

Subject Heading: FOOTBALL—FICTION / STUDENTS
Library of Congress Card Catalog Number: 99-32367

Library of Congress Cataloging-in-Publication Data
Bee, Clair.
  Freshman quarterback / by Clair Bee ; [edited by Cynthia
Bee Farley and Randall K. Farley].
    p. cm. — (The Chip Hilton sports series ; v. [9])
  Updated ed. of a work published in 1952.
  Summary: As a member of the freshman football team
at State University, Chip Hilton encounters cliques, rivalries,
and a conspiracy by the Booster Association to favor some
players over others.
  ISBN 0-8054-1991-8 (pbk.)
  [1. Football Fiction. 2. Sportsmanship Fiction. 3. Uni-
versities and colleges Fiction.] I. Farley, Cynthia Bee, 1952–
II. Farley, Randall K., 1952– . III. Title. IV. Series: Bee,
Clair. Chip Hilton sports series ; v. 9.
PZ7.B781955Fr 1999
[Fic]—dc21   99-32367
                  CIP
                  AC

1 2 3 4 5 03 02 01 00 99

The Chip Hilton Sports Series

For more information on
Chip Hilton-related activities and to correspond
with other Chip fans, check the Internet at
chiphilton.com

TO

THE LITTLEST INDIAN

Who inspired the writer long ago to play
the great game of football.

CLAIR BEE
1952

TO

JACK McCALLUM

The young stringer who followed his dream up a Roscoe mountain and
ended up rekindling the glory and magic of
Clair Bee and Chip Hilton.

Thank you,
RANDY AND CINDY FARLEY, 1999

Contents

CONTENTS

Foreword

WHEN I was ten or eleven years old, I was forced to read books by my parents. Since I liked athletes, I read and enjoyed several books by John R. Tunis that dealt primarily with baseball but also sportsmanship. Now fast forward to the summer of 1959, when at long last I had the opportunity to meet acclaimed basketball coach Clair Bee.

Frank McGuire was a close friend of Coach Bee, and I had just finished my first year as an assistant to Coach McGuire at North Carolina. Coach Bee was helping Frank with his basketball books, *Offensive Basketball* and *Defensive Basketball*. They had asked me to select two topics for chapters in *Defensive Basketball,* so we spent a great deal of time together that summer at the New York Military Academy.

During this period, not only did I stare at the painting of the fictional folk hero—Chip Hilton—that was on the wall behind Coach Bee's dining room table, but I had the opportunity to read some of the Chip Hilton series. The books were extremely interesting and well written, using sports as a vehicle to build character. No one did that better than Clair Bee (although Tunis came close). By that time, Bee's Chip Hilton books had become a classic series for youngsters. While Coach Bee was well known as one of the great coaches of all time due to his strategy and competitiveness, I believe he thought he could help society and young people most by writing this series. In his eyes, it was his "calling" in the years following his college and professional coaching career.

Coach McGuire and I, along with countless other basketball coaches, learned basketball from Clair Bee. The point zone, which Coach Bob Spear and I developed at the Air Force Academy, had its origins in one of Coach Bee's old books on the 1-3-1 rotating zone defense. We made our point zone at Air Force more of a match-up zone, but this is just one instance in which people on the basketball court today still depend on innovations by Clair Bee.

From 1959 until his death, I visited with Coach Bee frequently at the New York Military Academy and at Kutsher's Sports Academy, which he directed. He certainly touched my life as a special friend. Not only does he still rank at the top of his profession as a basketball coach, but he now regains the peak as a writer of sports fiction. I am delighted the Chip Hilton Sports series has been redone to make it more appropriate for athletics today without losing the deeper meaning of defining character. I encourage everyone to give these books as gifts to other young athletes so that Coach Bee's brilliant method of making sports come to life and building character will continue.

DEAN E. SMITH
Head Coach (Retired), Men's Basketball
University of North Carolina at Chapel Hill

CHAPTER 1

Freshman Flashes

WILLIAM "CHIP" HILTON could move! Chip could run the forty in full football gear in just about five seconds. He had never lost a sprint. Until now!

The tall quarterback's eyes bore into the big gold 41 on the white jersey stretched snugly across the broad back of the speeding runner ahead. It was the first time Chip had ever eaten dirt during a forty-yard sprint, and his eyes flickered desperately ahead to the goal line where Henry Rockwell, Nik Nelson, Jim Sullivan, and Curly Ralston waited for the finish.

Chip heard the thunder of pounding cleats behind him, but it was the rushing feet ahead that worried him, the flying legs of Fred "Fireball" Finley. Finley had led from the start, breaking away at Pete Pines's "Go!" as if snapped by a bungee cord. Everyone else had been fooled by the timing of the count and forced to get a late start.

Chip drifted slightly to the right and concentrated on the goal line ahead. This was the race of his freshman life, the first real college football test so far in the training camp's separation of the starters from the subs. Chip knew he'd have to make his move soon if he was going to win. Later, he'd figure out the reason for the strange timing of the starting signal. They were at the thirty now with Finley leading by two long strides. The gap didn't look that big . . . except to Chip, who was trying to close it up!

Chip's long legs were eating up the distance, streaking along in perfect rhythm. Ahead, Finley's powerful legs flashed mockingly over the green sod. At the twenty, Chip cut the lead to a single step. Then he furiously pumped his arms and increased his knee action. It paid off. He managed to pull even just before the two flashed across the goal line.

Finley cast a surprised glance at Chip as they slowed to a jog. "Where'd you come from?" he gasped. "If I'd known you were so close, I'd have opened up!"

Chip smiled. "I'll let you know next time," he said lightly.

Coach Nelson's whistle cut short further talk. Chip and the others surrounded the coaches on the goal line. Almost every panting player was grumbling about the starting signal.

"All right," Nelson bellowed, "let's have quiet! I'm sure you all know Coach Ralston. He's going to talk to you. Hit the bleachers! On the double, now!"

Chip turned and found Biggie Cohen, Red Schwartz, Speed Morris, and Soapy Smith beside him. The five Valley Falls friends trotted toward the bleachers in a tight little group.

"What kind of a deal was that?" Soapy demanded, jerking his head in Pete Pines's direction. "Finley was the only one who got away clean!"

"I don't know how you ever caught him," Speed added.

"Pines should've called us back," Schwartz complained.

"Maybe Pete wanted it that way," Biggie remarked dryly. "Maybe his bad ankle worked out good for his bud, Fireball Finley."

Chip said nothing. He was perplexed by several things that had happened since they had arrived at Camp Sundown. This race was just the latest in a number of incidents, and he was so absorbed that he never heard Nelson's first words, never heard him introduce State's new head varsity coach, the talk of the college football world. But that didn't mean that Chip didn't recognize Curly Ralston or didn't know all about him.

Curly Ralston was a presence. It was written in his keen, penetrating eyes, determined mouth, and strong, stubborn chin. His wide shoulders and long, tapering body would have challenged the physique of an Olympic champion. State's new varsity football coach was in his prime, both physically and professionally. Ralston was a nationally recognized football authority, a leader in techniques, and a respected educator. He had developed the winning habit in every program under his direction; Ralston was a coach of champion teams.

State University had interviewed a number of the country's leading football coaches and contacted several professional organizations before securing the famed coach's services.

Ralston was a powerful and inspiring speaker, and he was at his best when talking football. Standing in front of State's freshman hopefuls, Curly's penetrating voice carried clear and strong on the late summer air.

"Thanks, Coach Nelson. You and Coach Sullivan have a real squad here. Men, I guess you're getting into the swing of things by now. As you know, the drainage problems we faced on State's fields forced us to move down here to Camp Sundown for a few days, and we appreciate your flexibility. I must tell you that the coaching staff likes it so much here we just might decide to come again next year!

"Now you've attended your freshman student orientation and, of course, know your housing assignments. Your course registrations are complete and will be in your mailboxes when you return to campus. All in all, I'd say you're on your way. And I guess you've gotten pretty well acquainted with your coaches. Still, I'd like to tell you a little something about them and about Coach Henry Rockwell here.

"Coach Rockwell may be our newest member, but he's not unknown to State's coaching staff. The university, I understand, has been trying to get him up here for years. Coach Rockwell had originally been assigned to take full charge of all of State's freshman teams and particularly football. But a sudden resignation by one of our varsity staff members has changed all that, and we're pleased to have Coach Rockwell help out with the varsity. I might say, in passing, that no coach in the country can match the all-time victory record 'Rock' achieved at Valley Falls High School and no high school coach has ever developed so many impressive athletes.

"Rockwell players are known as great competitors. They're well coached and full of team spirit. We're fortunate to have him on our staff, and the varsity's gain is your loss—for now. Some of you will have a chance to work with Coach Rockwell next year on the varsity squad. Now, about the men who will work directly with you: This is Coach Nik Nelson's second year at State and he's been placed in charge. Coach Jim Sullivan is just like all of you—this is his rookie season. I'm sure you know about them. Both are State grads and had brilliant playing careers. They know the style of football we intend to use here at State, and you'll do well with them as your coaches. And now I'd like to talk a little football."

Ralston's voice changed. The words came crisply and with precision, both vibrant and penetrating. "I didn't like that race," he said flatly. "Football's a game of alertness, opportunism, quick thinking, and controlled action. That race degenerated into two heats, two sprints. The first was between Finley and Hilton! The other sprint was among the rest of the squad. We'll do that sprint again in a few minutes, and I want to see every one of you a contender this time. Speed is a football must.

"Now I'd like to give you a few ideas about our football philosophy here at State. First, a winning football team must have good players. They must be fast, aggressive, and smart. But that isn't enough! Powerful blocking, hard tackling, exceptional running, strong kicking, and expert passing are vital—but not enough. A team that is in first-class physical condition, efficiently equipped with offensive and defensive skills, and fighting all the way is a hard team to beat, but that *still* won't get the job done!"

Ralston shifted his position and took a few quick strides back and forth. He swung around, and his eyes swept the faces of the young men seated in the bleachers, their silent concentration focused on his every movement.

Then Ralston continued. "All of the qualities and abilities I've mentioned aren't enough unless the winning spirit is strong in each player's heart as an individual and as a member of the team. Spirit will do it! School spirit, team spirit, and loyalty to the spirit of the game. Without spirit, no team can or will ever be a great team.

"The varsity coaching staff takes pride in team spirit. We hope you'll take pride in team spirit too. And we hope you'll prove worthy of the confidence and loyalty you'll receive as the school's representatives. And another thing, the varsity coaching staff expects a lot from you as students and athletes. We'll be watching you as individuals and as a team to figure out just where you fit into our plans for next year. But remember, your most important focus should be on your education. Playing freshman football and hitting the books will give you that good start. Be sure you make good use of it.

"Well, I guess that's enough of a pep talk. Welcome to Camp Sundown and to State football." A broad smile spread across his lips and his eyes twinkled as he continued. "You're all probably aware that we have a pretty good crew practicing over there on the varsity field, and they've been talking about fresh meat for several days. I guess you know what that means—a scrimmage! So I've asked your coaches to have you ready for an unveiling Saturday afternoon at two o'clock."

State's varsity squad, which was practicing several hundred yards away, heard the roar that greeted Ralston's announcement. The enthusiasm the freshmen displayed as they tumbled down out of the bleachers and headed for the starting line at the goal must surely have convinced State's head coach that the rookies had plenty of spirit. It convinced Henry Rockwell. There was a lump in his throat, and he was glad he didn't have to do any talking right then. But the freshmen players were doing some talking about what they were going to do to the varsity on Saturday.

"We'll kill 'em!"

"You'd think he'd be afraid we'll hurt them!"

"By four touchdowns, easily!"

They quickly stopped the banter when Nik Nelson and Jim Sullivan yelled for them to line up for the sprint. If it had been later in the season, the coaches would have divided the squad, ends and backs in one group and linemen in another. But it was too early for that, too early to tell whether an athlete who had played guard in high school might not emerge as a blocking back, whether the tall halfback should not be shifted to end, even to a tackle slot. Kids grow up fast in college; hidden qualities and talents emerge hand-in-hand with a keen appreciation for their new responsibilities.

Pete Pines's whistle shrilled. Each player took his starting position on the goal line. Soapy Smith went into action then, stepping out of line.

"Hey, Pines," Soapy called, "how you gonna give the starting signal *this* time?"

"What d'ya mean?" Pines barked, glaring back at Soapy.

Biggie Cohen straightened up his six-foot-four-inch frame and placed his hands menacingly on his hips. "He means we were thrown off the first time by the break in cadence, Pines," Biggie said, his black eyes glittering angrily. "He didn't like it, and I didn't either! Get it?"

Pines feigned a glare of anger at Cohen for a long second, then turned abruptly around and retraced his steps. Pete had seen the beating the blocking sled took every time the big tackle's 235 pounds hit the target, and he knew what a bitter tackle could do to an end who antagonized him. In fact, before he'd gotten his bad ankle, he'd felt Biggie's hamlike hands several times when he tried to get under them to throw a block.

Pines lowered his eyes and retreated. "All right," he shouted over his shoulder, "we'll break after the count of three! On your mark!"

Chip dropped down in his starting position, lined up his path, and poised himself for the count.

"Get set! One! Two! Three! Go!

Chip's leg muscles tensed on the two count and he started his spring on Pines's "Three!" But the boy on Chip's left beat the count, slipped clumsily, and made a wild effort to regain his balance. At the last instant he grabbed Chip's shoulder and held on desperately. Chip never had a chance to get away and was forced to tear the boy's hand away. Straining to make up ground, he soon saw it was hopeless; he was too far behind.

Just before the end of the race, on the opposite twenty-yard line, he caught up with the last straining group as Finley crossed the goal line as the winner. Fireball had finished a scant three yards ahead of Speed Morris, but he slowed down quickly and waited for Chip to reach him.

"What happened, Hilton?" he jeered. "Miss the bus? Get tired? If you'd asked me, I would've given you a helping hand."

Chip grinned thinly. "No, Fireball," he replied softly, "I didn't get tired. I just wanted to see the whole race."

"How's the view from the back?"

"It won't happen again," Chip said coolly.

Once more Nelson's whistle ended all talk, and Chip trotted to a position in the big circle. His friends crowded around him.

"What happened?" Soapy whispered, perplexed.

"Nothing much," Chip murmured. "Just couldn't get started."

Directly across the circle, the boy who had grabbed Chip was whispering excitedly to Finley and Pete Pines. Fireball glanced directly at Chip and grinned sardonically. But Chip didn't return the taunt. He didn't want to believe what he was thinking—and he didn't think it was funny.

Nik Nelson paced back and forth in the center of the circle. His hard, raucous voice rang out sharply. "It's a little early for us to scrimmage, but you were instructed to report in shape, and we're proceeding on the theory that you're in condition. Just so we'll have some sort of teamwork, we'll select a couple of teams right now and work up some plays."

Nelson turned to Sullivan. "How do you want to make the teams, Coach?"

Sullivan glanced at the circle of players and nodded. "We've got a couple of pretty fair kickers here and since they're both quarterbacks . . ."

"Sure, that's it," Nelson agreed. "We'll let Finley and Hilton choose up. Come out here, you two. Finley, you and Hilton will be team captains. We'll run signals today, scrimmage tomorrow, rehearse plays on Friday, and beat the varsity Saturday afternoon! All right, Finley and Hilton, call a number, one to ten!"

"Four!" Fireball called quickly.

"Five!" Chip said.

Nelson's "eight" followed, and it was up to Chip. He hesitated, torn by loyalty to all four of his former Big Red friends before deciding to choose his friends alphabetically. "Cohen!"

Finley grinned. "Morris," he said deliberately, watching Chip intently.

"Schwartz," Chip said quietly.

"Smith!" Fireball barked triumphantly.

The exchange had not gone unnoticed. Each player and coach realized that this was the first challenge the camp had experienced. They knew that these two were taking the initiative, asserting their leadership because of their obvious abilities and because they were candidates for the same job.

As the two players faced each other, their teammates critically compared the taller Valley Falls star with his even more touted opponent. Chip's summer growth put him just over six feet three, weighing 185 pounds, but he looked almost skinny when compared to Finley. Fireball was an even six feet in height, but the 210 pounds he packed seemed to be concentrated in his shoulders and arms. There wasn't much doubt that the blue-eyed redhead was stronger.

But these collegiate players knew that modern football was no longer a game dominated by brute strength; they knew that speed, brains, spirit, and highly developed gridiron skills were more important.

Outsiders can never quite understand why two particular boys will emerge from a group as contenders for leadership. It is that indefinable something—part personality, part ability, part finer inner qualities—that is recognized only through close association and study. At any rate, teammates recognize the signs and apply their own standards in testing the candidates.

The players who arrived at Camp Sundown after State freshman orientation quickly recognized the possibilities of Fireball Finley and Chip Hilton. Almost overnight, it seemed, each quarterback had developed a following. The Valley Falls group showed right off the bat that Hilton was their leader. It was understandable. Chip had captained their high school team and was their best friend.

It was different with Finley. Fireball was an outsider, an out-of-state athlete with no following in camp. Yet from the start he'd been surrounded by and become the leader of what looked like a hand-picked all-star team.

Fireball's selection of Chip's hometown pals, Speed Morris and Soapy Smith, drew a few smirks of amusement. But Chip let it pass. He concentrated on selecting a good line.

"That one," Chip said, pointing to a tall player standing near Finley.

"Drew Carson," someone said.

"Rentler!" Fireball called.

"You," Chip countered, indicating the bulky teenager who had grabbed him at the start of the second sprint.

"Bebop Leopoulos," Carson told Chip, "plays center!"

And that's the way it went, Finley concentrating on backs and ends, Chip building a strong line, until the entire squad was divided.

"How about coaches?" someone asked.

"Good idea," Nelson agreed. "We'll let Finley and Hilton finger match for the choice. Ready, boys?" Finley called even on the hand thrust, and Chip won. Then Chip called "odds" and was again the winner. He hesitated momentarily and then chose Sullivan.

"Good!" Sullivan boomed. "A man after my own heart! Builds his team around the tackles! Come on, team. Let's go!"

Finley looked straight at Chip. "Guess I broke up the Valley Falls clique," he boasted.

Chip shot a quick glance at Speed and Soapy and caught the understanding in their eyes. Speed and Soapy would play their hearts out for Fireball's team, but it would take more than a scrimmage to break up their friendship. Even the great game of football wasn't big enough to do that!

CHAPTER 2

Booster Treatment

FOOTBALL WEATHER is exhilarating for everyone. Players and coaches paw the ground like restless race horses, enthusiastic fans jam the stadiums early for tailgate parties, and stripe-shirted officials display a calm demeanor while excitedly anticipating the kickoff. It's a great feeling!

It was a perfect football day. Crisp enough to add zip, clear enough to provide the azure backdrop for a high, spiraling ball, just warm enough to keep the spectators comfortable.

Yes, there were spectators, lots of them, even for this intrasquad freshman game. Curly Ralston was giving his varsity squad a breather and brought them along to watch the scrimmage. There were some parents, alumni, and local sportswriters in the stands too.

Out on the field, the players were going through their warm-up drills under the watchful eyes of Nik Nelson and Jim Sullivan. Henry Rockwell, Curly Ralston, and several varsity assistants stood in a little knot on the sideline.

Chip was thrilled clear to his toes when Jim Sullivan sent him to do some kicking. Stavros "Bebop" Leopoulos covered the ball, and McGuire and Anderson trotted downfield to receive the kicks. Directly opposite, on the thirty-five-yard line, Finley began booting the ball too. Fireball could kick all right, and he wasted no time loosening up. His boots, traveling low and spinning hard, averaged fifty yards.

Curly Ralston elbowed Rockwell and nodded toward the stands. "There's B. G. Anderson, the head of the Booster Club. I've heard he's all business. Everyone calls him 'Biz.' People say he's pretty powerful around here too. He claims Finley's the greatest freshman prospect he ever saw, says every school in the country was after him. He raves about his kicking."

A quick smile flitted across Rockwell's lips. Then he gestured toward Chip Hilton. "Biz Anderson never saw Chip boot 'em," he said softly. "Wait a couple minutes and you'll see."

But there wasn't much to see. Bebop Leopoulos took care of that. His snaps came back low and to the right, high and to the left, came back like a bullet one time, floated back like a balloon the next. Chip's timing was completely thrown off, and his kicks finished a poor second to Finley's beautiful spirals.

"How long does it take him to loosen up?" Ralston asked dryly.

"Something's not right," Rockwell answered quickly. "Must still be tight."

"Could be," Ralston said thoughtfully. "Well, let's get this thing going. OK, Nik," he called. "Let's go!"

Seconds later, Chip was facing Finley in the center of the field. Four white-knickered, stripe-shirted officials flanked them. "All right," the referee said crisply, "we're playing four fifteen-minute quarters, regular football."

FRESHMAN QUARTERBACK

He poised a coin in his hand. "One of you call it."

"Heads!" Fireball cried.

Heads it was and Finley chose to receive.

"We'll defend the east goal," Chip said. "Good luck, Finley!"

Sullivan was waiting in the huddle of players when Chip reported. "Good!" the burly coach said aggressively. "We've got the wind. Let's see what those running backs can do without some protection up in front of 'em. Think you can kick it over the goal, Hilton?"

Chip nodded. "Coach, with that wind I can kick it out of the end zone!"

That was what Chip thought. But he had overlooked Lonnie Akins. Akins was holding the ball on the tee. Chip took his seven backward steps, raised his arms, and started the forward charge. Everything was smooth and comfortable until Chip's leg thrust started his kicking toe for the spot on the ball. Right then, Akins jerked his hand away from the ball, and the toe of Chip's kicking shoe struck the pigskin half-true. The result was a wobbly and weak thirty-yard kick that a surprised Dave English gathered joyfully in his arms and carried to the forty before he was downed. So it was Finley's ball on his own forty, first and ten.

Both teams had been equipped with the T-formation and the same plays. Finley took the quarterback position, confident that he had the best backs. He sent Wells into the line, but Donnell ran into a stone wall and didn't gain an inch. Then he tried Robert "Speed" Morris around right end, but again Chip's superior line smothered the play. Fireball had lost some of his confidence when he joined his teammates in the huddle, but he was stubborn and ignored their pleas for a flare pass to Speed swinging wide out of the backfield.

"Look," Fireball insisted, "we've got good receivers. We'll try a long pass."

That was a mistake. Biggie Cohen, Bob Dean, and Bo Gilmore were right on Finley's heels; they easily broke through the line and threw Fireball for a ten-yard loss. They did the same thing on the next play, blocking the punt. Cohen recovered the ball for Chip's team on the twenty-yard line.

Chip hustled into the huddle and called the play. "We'll keep 'em on the run, guys! Anderson in motion and Roberts over 'four' on the count of three! Let's go, Roberts!"

Roberts didn't go anywhere. Chip took his position behind Leopoulos, gave the count, felt just enough of the ball on the snap to know it was a fumble, and then found himself on his back, snowed under an avalanche of players. The referee dug into the freshman pile and patted English on the back. It was Finley's ball, first and ten on the twenty-five.

"What happened?" Roberts growled.

Chip didn't reply, turned abruptly, and trotted back to his position. He wasn't talking because he was doing some keen thinking. First the punting . . . then the kick-off . . . now the very first play of the scrimmage . . .

There was nothing good about that scrimmage for Chip. When the snap from Leopoulos was good, Roberts or McGuire fumbled. When he passed to anyone but Schwartz, the receiver fumbled, turned the wrong way, or the trailing back completely missed the pitch. When he went back to kick, the whole line seemed to crumble, except on the left side where Schwartz and Cohen were operating at left end and tackle. But the center and right side of the line were a sieve; Chip never had a chance. He was being hammered by his own hand-picked team.

Two of the three kicks he attempted were blocked, and the one he managed to get away flubbed off his foot for a mere thirty yards. Eventually, Sullivan took him out and sat him out for the rest of the game. Things were better then, it seemed, and his teammates managed to tie it up at 13-all in the last quarter.

Chip dressed slowly, almost numb in his despair. He couldn't understand it. Like everyone else, he'd wanted to make a good showing in the scrimmage. But this wasn't funny—the teasing had a decidedly mean edge to it.

Chip was puzzled, too, by the attitude of Finley's clique. He couldn't understand their spiteful treatment. Until four days ago, he'd never even heard of Fireball or Bebop or Pines or Akins!

Chip would have understood a lot of things if he could have overheard the conversation that evening between Coach Nik Nelson and the president of State's Booster Association, Biz Anderson. On the way to dinner at the Pomeroy House in the neighboring town of Rocky River, the two men discussed the freshman team.

"How are the kids shaping up?" Anderson asked.

"It's a little early to tell, Mr. Anderson," Nelson answered slowly, "but most of the Booster crew look good."

"Most of them?" Anderson echoed.

Nelson hesitated. "Well," he replied cautiously, "there's some more or less unknowns out there who look pretty good."

"That's strange," Anderson said. "You mean they're better than the Booster players?"

"Two or three."

"I don't understand that! I thought we got every single freshman on the list. We'll certainly look foolish if they don't make good. Remember, they're expected to be a big part of next year's varsity. That's why we involved ourselves in this program."

"Oh, they'll make good all right," Nelson began. "That is—"

"That is, what?"

"If Ralston keeps Rockwell with the varsity."

"What's that got to do with it?"

"Nothing much," Nelson continued uncertainly, "except that I don't think Rockwell knows the Boosters' relationship to the freshman pilot program. He's sure pulling for those Valley Falls players. And I'm not sure Ralston completely understands the whole situation either."

"How the members of the association utilize their own resources is none of their business," Anderson snapped. "What about the Valley Falls kids?"

"Rockwell coached them so it's natural for him to be high on their ability."

"And you?"

"In my opinion, there's at least two who'd be starting on the varsity right now if State hadn't joined this freshman pilot program with the national athletic association."

"Which two?"

"The tall, blond quarterback and the big tackle, Hilton and Cohen. The Booster recruiters might've missed a couple of others too."

"You think this Hilton might have something?"

Nelson nodded grimly. "That's an understatement. If you were an alumnus, you'd know this Hilton kid's dad was one of the greatest athletes in State's history. Played three sports. The kid looks like a natural too."

"Then I don't see how we missed him," Anderson wondered.

"That's easy," Nelson replied. "The Booster Association only had the previous coach's list of incoming freshmen who'd signed letters of intent and were offered scholarships before the university decided to go with the freshman pilot program. Hilton and Cohen weren't on that list, so they were walk-ons, unknown to the association."

"If they're that good, then why didn't State's coaches go after them?"

"Don't know about Cohen, but I hear that in high school Hilton told Rockwell he was going to State like his dad and paying his own way. Wasn't interested in the recruiting process. He must have gotten calls and letters from all over the place to play football. Just wasn't interested. Imagine that."

"So you think this Hilton and Cohen and a couple of the others are better than some of the Booster kids?"

Nelson nodded decisively. "Yes, I do. You know, they sort of prove Dad Young's argument. He wanted to concentrate on students, especially freshmen, getting a solid foundation. He felt too many athletes failed to graduate because they were expected to perform on the field and weren't able or ready to cope with the classroom demands of a university. Guess that's why Dad considered resigning as athletic director. At least that's the way I got the story."

Anderson shrugged his shoulders. "That could be right," he said. "So what?"

"Well, when the pilot program was created, he jumped at the chance to involve State," Nelson concluded. "It's OK by me, I guess—I've got no complaints. I figure the association is helping some players."

"And got you a job coaching," Anderson added softly.

"That's right."

"I gather you think the Booster kids will make it tough for anyone else to break in."

Nelson chuckled. "You notice anything this afternoon?"

"Not particularly. Why?"

"Well, the Booster kids have stuck together ever since the dinner last Saturday. They know how they stand, and they're going to protect their own interests and the interests of each other."

"Who's the leader?"

"Looks like Finley. Anyway, when this Hilton kid began to look too good, Finley challenged him, and the Booster crew backed up Fireball. They sure gave Hilton a rough time and made him look bad."

"How?"

"Oh, bad passes, fumbles, poor blocking, missed assignments . . ."

"What about Hilton? He catch on?"

"Only that he wasn't getting cooperation."

"How did he react?"

"Just kept his head and kept trying. What else *could* he do?"

"Nothing much, I guess," Anderson said reflectively. "By the way, how's Eddie doing?"

"Good, Mr. Anderson. He's going to be all right with a little work."

Anderson laughed. "Work! That kid of mine doesn't know what the word means. Wish he did! He's been moody this last year. Not too much fighting spirit, I guess. I'd hoped he'd catch on with some of these football players and change for the better. It looks to me as though you've got a tough job on your hands. Guess there isn't a Booster in the association who doesn't think the player he's sponsoring will be the next Heisman winner."

"Don't worry, Mr. Anderson. Everything will work out all right as long as Rockwell stays with the varsity."

"I think that can be arranged," Anderson said pointedly. "Remember, the Booster Association has gone to a lot of trouble to help these players. We've invested in them, and we need to see a return on that investment."

Chip Hilton was the topic of conversation that night. Most of the freshmen were watching football videos. But half a dozen had gathered in Fireball Finley's cabin where Bebop Leopoulos was doing most of the talking.

"You should've seen his face when I grabbed him," Leopoulos chuckled. "He looked at me like I was crazy."

"He was right!" Roberts quipped.

"Now you behave," Bebop chided good-naturedly.

"He can run," Sean Reynolds said seriously. "I think he's the fastest man on the squad."

"No way!" Leopoulos growled.

"Then why did you have to hold him?" Reynolds asked.

Leopoulos couldn't answer that, and there was a brief silence. Each player was engrossed in thought.

"Well, I know a kicker when I see one," Fireball admitted reluctantly. "Hilton is one of the best."

"Not when I'm centering the ball," Leopoulos beamed. "Did I keep him off balance? High snaps, low snaps—had him going crazy!"

"I'm surprised he let you get away with it," McGuire said thoughtfully.

"You should talk!" Bebop retorted. "You made him look bad every time he handled the ball."

"Yeah, and I don't feel too good about it," McGuire retorted. "Period!"

BOOSTER TREATMENT

Fireball Finley summed it up. "I don't think any of us feel too good about it. Maybe we're carrying this treatment too far. I didn't come here to gang up on anyone. I came to get an education and play football!"

"Yeah, right!" Reynolds said shortly. "But haven't you forgotten something?"

A wave of red slowly rose over Finley's face. "You mean the association?" he demanded. "Sure, I like the treatment I get. Why not?"

CHAPTER 3

Famous or Infamous?

CAMP SUNDOWN didn't offer much free time for the one hundred or so football players who had reported. Not that the varsity candidates or freshman hopefuls were disappointed. The long grass drills, tackling dummy sessions, killing contact-work of the mornings, *and* the sheer drudgery of three hours of starts, stops, sprints, pass chasing, punt covering, and signal running in the hot afternoons tempered all desire for extracurricular activity. Almost as tiring were the after-dinner skull-practice sessions that no one missed.

Most of the players received letters earlier in the summer advising them to report in condition. But it takes real courage to train during the lazy, summer vacation weeks, and only a few had paid the price. So, as was to be expected, the three-hour long practice stints were taking their toll, keeping the trainers busy every minute with what they mockingly called "ouchies," "boo-boos," and a few real injuries.

FAMOUS OR INFAMOUS?

Chip had his own method for eliminating the stiffness that gripped every muscle in his body. Every morning before breakfast he would grab a basketball and wander over to the outdoor court closest to his cabin to practice shooting. Shooting hoops loosens up the kinks without the player even realizing it, especially if he likes basketball. Chip loved the game and so did his Valley Falls buddies. With the exception of Biggie Cohen, they had played together all through high school.

It wasn't long before other freshmen began to show up, and the inevitable resulted—a full-court game. The competition naturally drew spectators, and with every workout Chip's hoop stature grew. But his football abilities seemed to have been overlooked, lost in the shuffle.

Nelson and Sullivan concentrated on T-formation plays and defensive formations in both of Friday's practice sessions, and that night they used a wide-screen TV to analyze a video of one of State's big games of the previous year. They were very thorough, rewinding, slowing down, or freezing the action on specific frames from time to time while they talked about blocking assignments, pass protection, and rushing techniques. The two coaches treated the coming varsity encounter as if it were a championship game, and their spirit gradually enveloped the whole squad.

Later, and long into the night, the two coaches sat in their cabin discussing plans for the next afternoon.

"A week just isn't enough," Sullivan declared forcefully.

"You're right!" Nelson agreed. "You know something! I've got a feeling Curly's worried. He's got some tough games early in the season, and I don't believe he thinks the varsity's got what it takes."

Sullivan grunted in agreement. "I know they haven't got it! That's the reason for tomorrow's scrimmage. We're being served up to the varsity. Curly knows *we're* not ready."

"Well, we're as close to it as humanly possible, with the little time we've had. Let's run over the roster again. Guess we won't have much of a chance to see what talent we really have with all those Booster Association members in the stands waiting for their special players to be in on every play. We'll have to use the players the association coddles, whether we want to or not."

"Only change I see is to shift Kornowitz to left tackle and move Dean over to end in place of Pines."

Nelson pursed his lips and shrugged his shoulders. "That's the best we can do unless we use Cohen." He shook his head hopelessly. "And if we do that, we'll have every Booster on our backs."

"They'll all be here," Sullivan said ruefully. "You can be sure of *that*."

Nelson was silent for a long minute. "You know something?" he demanded suddenly. "If Cohen isn't the best lineman out there, I'll eat Rockwell's old cap. You know what Cohen would probably do if we used him? Ruin the whole right side of Curly's line."

Sullivan grinned. "Yeah, and then you and I could start looking for other jobs. Let's have another look at that squad, Nik."

"Leopoulos at center, Akins and Gilmore at the guards, Kornowitz and Maxim at the tackles, Dean and Reynolds at the ends. Finley at quarter, McGuire and Rentler at the halves, and Roberts at full. Guess that's it!"

"Your guess is as good as mine. Outside of Hilton, Cohen, Morris, English, and Anderson, I don't know one from the other."

FAMOUS OR INFAMOUS?

"I can't see Anderson!" Sullivan said decisively. "He's a long way from being ready. I'll say one thing for him though. He's got guts and he sure gives it all he's got."

Nelson grinned sardonically. "Can you see his old man if Anderson played against the varsity?"

"A player stands on his own two feet in football. Besides," Sullivan added quickly, "I know enough about Eddie Anderson to know that he'd quit football if he thought his father was using influence so he could play. Eddie's a sensitive kid, and he knows exactly where he stands. Well, I've had enough football for one day. Tomorrow's a big day!"

Saturday dawned bright and clear, and most of the freshmen spent the morning leisurely hanging out around the sports camp, talking about the game, all the while trying not to let their game-day butterflies show. It was a big event for all of them, a milestone in their progress toward gaining a starting spot on the new freshman team. And what was just as important, a chance to prove what they were made of to the other members of the squad.

The small north sideline bleachers were filled by one o'clock. And when the freshman and varsity squads trotted out on the field thirty minutes later, the south sideline was packed with anxious, proud Boosters who were ready to take the credit for State's rookie phenoms, surely next year's all-Americans.

The varsity wore State's traditional red-and-blue uniforms with white helmets, while the freshmen wore white jerseys, nondescript pants, and red headgear.

Chip ran through signals with the freshman reserve players. His heart was heavy, but his actions belied his feelings. The clear, forceful tone of his voice gave his teammates a lift, snapped them into a cohesive unit, instilled in them a feeling of confidence and assurance. When the pregame kicking began, it imbued Dave English with some sort of sudden comradeship too. Dave had never spoken two words to Chip before, but he grabbed a ball now and called to Chip, Speed Morris, and Eddie Anderson.

"Come on, Chip, show 'em up! Morris, you and Anderson chase 'em!"

English centered the ball, and the passes came back sure and fast. Right where Chip liked them, every time. This was what Chip had been waiting for, and every kick was a protest against the treatment he had received.

Standing even with Fireball, Chip sent his booming punts boring high into the air, spinning aloft until they nose-dived wickedly down. Each one carried ten to twenty yards beyond Fireball's efforts. It was beautiful to see, and, as Chip warmed up, Morris and Anderson were chased farther and farther back until the spiraling punts were averaging sixty to seventy yards.

Henry Rockwell, standing beside Curly Ralston, couldn't resist a chuckle, elbowed the head coach, and nodded across the field. "There. See what I mean?" he queried.

Ralston nodded. "Who couldn't see those boomers!" he said approvingly. "Nothing wrong with his leg today."

Even the Boosters couldn't possibly miss that kicking performance, and they quizzed one another until they heard the name of the novice blond punter.

"Hilton! Never heard of him! Who's his sponsor?"

"Valley Falls? Oh, right here in the state!"

"I never saw any freshman kick a ball like that!"

"He's had some special coaching along the way. There's an educated toe if there ever was one!"

Fireball Finley couldn't take the competition. He told Leopoulos he'd had enough and trotted off the field. Chip called it quits then too. He'd gotten something off his chest. Besides, it wasn't as tough as he'd thought sitting on the bench a few minutes later would be.

Only Chip didn't sit. He wasn't made that way. He was on his feet, the first to cheer his freshman team-mates as they broke from the huddle and trotted out on the field to receive the kickoff. The Boosters cheered too. They had been waiting weeks to see this freshman "Wonder Team" unveiled. They were especially eager to see Fireball Finley, who was tabbed by the local press as the high school sensation of the country.

Fireball Finley electrified the crowd the very first play. Taking the kickoff on the fifteen-yard line, he took off twisting, turning, and bullying his way to midfield before he was brought down. Every Booster was on his feet, cheering the sensational run. But the run and the cheers only served to fill the varsity with resentment, which promptly proceeded to put the so-called wonder boys in their place. They held the freshmen three straight times for no gain and then took over on their own twenty-yard line when Finley's punt bounded into the end zone. They then rolled on for three straight touchdowns and three straight two-point conversions, taking the ball away from the hapless freshman team each time without allowing them to gain a yard.

Near the end of the second quarter, with the varsity leading 24-0, a large, well-dressed man with football shoulders sauntered out on the sidelines and sat down beside Nelson on the bench. "Hi ya, Nik," he said famil-iarly. "Not doin' so good!"

"Hi ya, Hunk," Nelson said coolly. "We're not ready, that's all."

"Don't worry about it, Nik. Say, why don't you give Biz Anderson's kid a look? Biz would give his right arm to see the kid out there in the scrimmage. Go on, put him in."

Nelson glanced resignedly at Sullivan and then called Anderson. "Eddie, go in for Rentler. On the double now!"

Anderson looked up with surprise. "Me? Why," he began, "I—"

"Stop stuttering!" Nelson said sharply. "I said go in for Rentler." He turned abruptly away, concentrated on the players, and didn't even glance up when the visitor said good-bye and left the bench.

Eddie Anderson slowly picked up a helmet and waited for the whistle. Reluctantly, he trotted out and ducked into the huddle. The substitution meant a measure of pleasure for Biz Anderson, but it brought only embarrassment to his son. Eddie stood five feet eight and weighed a solid 170 pounds, but he was dwarfed by the other freshmen on the field and looked almost fragile. Eddie knew exactly where he stood when compared to Chip Hilton or Speed Morris or any one of three or four other backfield candidates. But he loved football and as soon as the play started, he forgot all about everything but the game.

The varsity players continued to pour it on and scored again before the end of the half, leaving the field with a 31-0 bulge. In the second half, they appeared to be taking it easy, scoring only once in the third quarter. But they made sure the highly touted freshmen didn't move the ball, pinning them deep in their own territory with superior, well-placed kicking. The varsity's big ends covered Finley like a blanket.

Late in the last quarter, the varsity punted out of bounds on the freshman fifteen and after two downs for the usual no-gain, Nelson called Chip's name. "All right,

FAMOUS OR INFAMOUS?

Hilton, in for Finley! Cohen for Kornowitz, Morris for Anderson, Schwartz and Smith at the ends. Hurry now!"

Chip, thrilling at the chance, dashed into the huddle and called for a pass. But his hopes were blasted once again by Leopoulos. Bebop thrust the ball back just as far as Chip's finger tips and then held the ball. The varsity line charged, and the ball bounced right at Chip's feet and rolled back to the five-yard line.

It seemed as though there were fifty men chasing him, but Chip fell on the ball and hung on with all his might, even though several of the varsity linemen tried to wrestle the precious prize out of his arms. But his heart was sick. The referee slapped Chip on the back, and he hopped up and scurried back into the end zone for the huddle. Chip's jaw was set now. If this was the way it had to be, he'd meet it that way.

Speed Morris was looking at him with inquiring eyes. Chip nodded and grabbed the fleet back by the arm. "Big Red 69, Speed," he muttered savagely. "Get it?"

Morris looked blank an instant, then nodded grimly and whispered something to Soapy Smith. In the huddle Chip called for punt formation. "We'll kick," he said crisply. "On three!"

Before anyone could move, Chip leaned forward and tapped Leopoulos on the chest. "Don't bounce the ball back, Bebop," he said pointedly. "Throw it! OK, guys. Let's go!"

"You hear what he said, Leopoulos?" Cohen demanded roughly as they broke out of the huddle.

Leopoulos nodded sullenly, and Chip saw Soapy and Schwartz break apart at the line of scrimmage.

Chip took his time getting set in the end zone and then started the count. The ball came spinning back on "three" and Chip faked the kick, tricking his freshman teammates as well as the varsity. Speed threw a beautiful block on the hard-charging end, and Biggie lowered the boom on State's big right tackle. It was routine then for Chip to fade to his left and zip a perfect peg to Schwartz at the thirty-yard line. Red gathered in the toss without breaking stride and was down to the fifty-yard stripe before two varsity players knocked him out of bounds.

In the huddle Chip apologized. "I had to do it, guys. Sorry, won't happen again. Regular formation now, fake pass-buck, 47. On two! Let's—"

Cohen checked him. "Hold it a sec, Chip," Biggie drawled. "I want to explain something to Bebop." He placed a heavy arm over the surly center's shoulders. "Look, Bebop," he said patiently, "the ball's supposed to be placed into the quarterback's hands and left there. Get it?" Biggie tightened his arm around Leopoulos's neck and smiled convincingly. "You understand, my friend, don't you?"

Leopoulos shrugged Cohen's arm away and nodded, and Biggie turned back to Chip. "OK, Chipper," he said sweetly. "Bebop understands the game of football perfectly now."

Leopoulos was evidently impressed by Cohen's advice, because the ball slapped surely and swiftly into Chip's hands on the count. Chip gave the charging varsity line a lesson in sleight-of-hand wizardry on that play, pivoting away from Bebop and seemingly faking the ball to hard-driving Speed Morris. Then Chip faked again to McGuire and dashed back with his right arm and hand concealed behind his right leg. All the time he was dancing about and looking downfield as though searching for a receiver.

The line hit him then, but as he went down, Chip saw Speed streaking toward the sideline twenty yards downfield. It was beautiful. Morris nearly got away but finally was pulled down on the varsity fifteen-yard line. On the next play, Chip called the alternate, again faking the pass. This time McGuire made a seven-yard gain, and it was second and three.

The varsity massed on the line, figuring the obvious. Chip ran the same play, and the desperate varsity line tackled both Morris and McGuire. But this time Chip kept the ball and rifled a bullet pass smack into Smith's stomach just as Soapy buttonhooked in the end zone. Seconds later, with Morris holding, Chip split the crossbar for the extra point.

The freshmen had scored in exactly two minutes on five plays, and the Boosters gave the kids a big hand as they trotted back up the field. The varsity lined up to receive, determined to run the kickoff all the way, but Chip spoiled that. He kicked the ball into the end zone and out of bounds. Then the revived freshman line dug in and held the varsity three straight times.

Chip hurried back to his own thirty-five and waited for the punt, hoping the kicker would kick straightaway. He got his wish. The ball was high, yards short of his position, but Chip didn't move. He gave the flanking ends a good focal point and felt a joyful tingle in his chest as they angled for him at full speed. Just as the ball nosed down, Chip set his arms for the catch and looked up, faking for all he was worth. That was enough for the ends, and they turned on the speed, anticipating a good hit on this freshman receiver. Then Chip broke for the ball and took it on the forty-four. The ends had fallen for the trick; they couldn't change direction quickly enough, and Chip was away with only the varsity center and left tackle as immediate problems.

Speed dumped the center with a neat block, and Chip cut to the left, easily outrunning the tackle. Biggie Cohen had taken care of the varsity right tackle, and Chip easily faked the varsity punter with a stutter step; with a clear field he then went all the way. That made it 38-13. Seconds later it was 38-14, thanks to Chip's perfect placement.

Fireball Finley and a whole new team came trotting out then, and Chip headed for the bench, feeling better than he had at any time since he had arrived at Camp Sundown.

Finley kicked off, and the varsity had time to make two quick first downs before the scrimmage ended.

Breathing deep sighs of relief, Nelson and Sullivan started across the field toward Ralston. But they never reached the head coach. They were intercepted by Biz Anderson, Ned Calvin, and several other alumni quarterbacks, all angry and talkative.

"What was the idea of pulling out Finley and Kornowitz and Rentler and Reynolds when the varsity was all worn out?"

"Yeah, and what was the idea of playing Dean at end?"

"Pines is the best young pass receiver in the country! Where was he?"

"Look, Nelson, those players have to play! That's why they're here, and we don't want to lose them!"

"Yeah, they came here to play football, not to ride the bench!"

"You've got to keep them happy, and happy is playing."

There was more, but Nelson and Sullivan didn't remember much of it. They heard the words, but the hot blood of anger surged to the surface. Later, as the freshman coaches met in their cabin, the bitter thoughts burst forth in angry conversation.

FAMOUS OR INFAMOUS?

"They think they own us!" Nelson stormed. "I'd like to tell them all to jump in the lake!"

"We don't owe them a thing, Nik. We played four years of football, graduated, and did our best. What else do they expect?"

"Bow every time they look sideways, I guess."

"Forget this! There must be easier ways to begin a coaching career!"

"You said a mouthful. I'm fed up with State's famous Booster Association."

"Famous or infamous?" Sullivan asked bitterly.

CHAPTER 4

Prima Donnas

THE SUV was a beauty. The long, trim, red metal-flaked body and gold alloy wheels spelled speed and class. Chip sighed, took one last look, and then turned back to take another shot at the basket.

"Not bad, is it?"

Chip swung around in surprise. He had been so absorbed in admiring the sport utility vehicle that he had not seen Eddie Anderson approaching.

"It's a beauty," Chip agreed enthusiastically. "Must have cost a lot."

"Even has a power sunroof and six-disc CD changer," Eddie said shortly. "The owner can afford it though," he added quickly.

"You know him?"

Eddie smiled ruefully. "Sometimes I wonder," he said gloomily. "He's my dad."

Chip caught the dejection in Eddie's voice and immediately went into action. "Catch," he said, snapping a crisp bounce pass toward Eddie as he cut for the basket. The return pass relieved the tension, and they were soon busy matching shots around the court.

Ten minutes later, a tall man and Fireball Finley came out of one of the cabins and hopped in the red SUV. Fireball was at the wheel, but Chip paid no attention, concentrating instead on his shooting. Eddie concentrated, too, but he lost interest soon after the vehicle roared away.

"Think I'll take off now, Chip," he said more dejectedly than when he had arrived. "It's been great . . ."

It was the first time Anderson had ever spoken Chip's nickname. The tall, blond quarterback was surprised, but he recovered quickly. "It sure has, Eddie. Let's do it again. Want to join us in the morning? A couple of us come up here and shoot around every morning before breakfast."

An appreciative smile spread across Anderson's lips. "Thanks, Chip. Thanks a lot."

Chip watched his new friend walk slowly toward the cabins and then resumed his shooting. But Eddie's evident gloom had left its mark. Chip could no longer concentrate. After taking a string of unsuccessful shots, he made a final basket and then headed to the cabin to get ready for dinner.

Nelson and Sullivan were getting ready for dinner too. They had surprised B. G. Anderson by declining his invitation to join the Boosters and their protégés for dinner in Antlers, choosing instead to remain at the camp and eat with the rest of the freshman squad. They were still stinging from the scolding received earlier, but the two coaches were sincere when they told the president of the Boosters Association that they felt they'd better stick around. "The kids left in camp will think everyone's walked out on them," Nelson said.

"We thought about inviting everyone," Anderson had explained lamely, "but you see we have to bring some of the Boosters and the players they've taken under their wings together some way and—"

"We understand," Nelson assured him coolly.

The freshman dining tables that night were strangely quiet. Nelson and Sullivan tried to lighten the mood but had little success. The Booster stars had been openly jubilant and excited about leaving camp for dinner, and the players who remained were adding two and two together. The sum revealed the significant fact that only the so-called reserves had been left behind.

After the football videos, the whole group trooped along behind Chip, following him to the "Valley Falls" cabin just as if it had been prearranged. The inevitable bull session followed.

"How come you didn't go to town, Anderson?" Kip Waldorf asked pointedly.

"I wasn't asked," Anderson replied calmly. "In fact, I wouldn't have gone if I had been asked."

"You mean your old man didn't invite *you?*" Kip persisted.

Eddie laughed. "That's right! No one sponsors my football except myself. I don't need someone to pamper me."

"Just what does all this Booster stuff mean, Eddie?" English asked.

"Just about what it sounds like, Dave. Some members of the Booster Association look out for certain athletes in football, basketball, and baseball—especially this year with State's new pilot program where freshman can play only on freshman teams."

"From what I hear the Boosters try to run the whole athletic program," Montague said sourly.

"They think they do! I think they're afraid some of their stars will leave for other schools if they don't get some special treatment. Only they call it mentoring."

"Wish I had a mentor," Soapy said dreamily. "I deserve a lot of special attention. And hey! That reminds me! I gotta get a job! How's a guy go about finding a part-time job at school, Eddie?"

"Best bet's through the university's career services."

"I've got to find one too," Chip ventured. "I guess they aren't too plentiful in a college town."

"There's more than you'd think," Anderson assured Chip. "Of course, a lot depends on what you can do. Most of the students who have to work get campus spots like the cafeteria or the library; some work at fast food places, gas stations, or convenience stores."

"I'm a trained, expertly qualified food and beverage customer liaison. You know, a maitre d' of burgers, fries, and shakes—an old-fashioned soda jerk!" Soapy announced proudly. "So's Chip!"

Red Schwartz murmured something, and Soapy looked at him suspiciously. "What'd you say?" Soapy demanded.

"I agreed with you," a sly, smiling Schwartz explained. "That's all."

That did it! Soapy tangled with Schwartz, and the two friends lurched and staggered all over the cabin, uttering direful threats and managing somehow to fall all over Montague and English. The newcomers took it seriously until Biggie and Speed pulled the two pranksters apart, and they all began to laugh.

Later, as he was leaving, Anderson talked briefly with Chip and Soapy. He knew a man in University who often hired college students to work in his place. "I'll drop in to see him and put in a good word for you," he assured the ex-Sugar Bowl duo. "He's a longtime friend of our family. Has a nice business. It's the same kind of place you guys worked at in Valley Falls—only bigger and busier. Lots of the students hang out there."

After lights out, the Valley Falls cabin quieted down with only Soapy's usual affected buzz-saw snoring disturbing the silence. That ended after a time too. Chip tossed restlessly, but sleep just wouldn't come. Eventually, he resigned himself to the fact and thought the problem through. He knew where he stood now, and he guessed Biggie and Speed and Soapy and Red and the rest of them knew where they stood too. One thing was sure. The stars were going to find the going rough from here on in!

And rough it was! On everyone! Nelson and Sullivan drove the squad through the long morning and afternoon workouts without mercy. Grass drills, sprints, group blocking, charging sleds, and tackling-dummy drudgery in the mornings; running signals, chasing punts, live tackling, slow-motion work on plays, kickoff drills, pass defense, and scrimmage in the afternoons. The men were being separated from the boys, fast! Every morning two or three candidates were suddenly called home for a final visit or managed to self-diagnose season-ending "ouchies," "boo-boos," or flare-ups of old high school football wounds. Most of the walk-ons discovered one excuse was just as good as another.

Nelson and Sullivan had the slackers tabbed. Some of the Booster stars knew every trick in the book; they knew a pulled back muscle or rib injury was difficult to check. Through it all, the Valley Falls group and Eddie Anderson worked hard at every practice and through every drill. Surprisingly, Fireball Finley seemed to like the rough going.

Then it was Friday night, and everyone puttered around, packing and talking about the varsity scrimmage the next morning and the breakup of preseason workouts afterward. It would be the last weekend off before the first day of fall semester classes . . . and more football practice. The Valley Falls crowd was talking about home, the Sugar Bowl, and Petey Jackson, John Schroeder, Speed's Mustang, Doc Jones, and their college plans.

"You think the Mustang can make it, Speed?" Soapy asked.

"Make it?" Morris retorted. "That's an insult!"

"The Morris wheels will be here," Biggie said confidently. "So will Petey!"

"You sold your car to Petey?" Soapy blurted.

"No way, man! Since freshmen can't have cars on campus, we've got an agreement; he gets to use the car my freshman year, and he has to drive me and my selected guests back and forth from school when we get breaks."

"Class, all class. That's what I call it," Soapy said grandly.

"What d'ya say, you guys?" Schwartz pleaded. "Let's get a good night's rest. We're scrimmaging the varsity in the morning. Remember?"

"We?" Soapy griped sarcastically. "You have a wonderful imagination, my fine football friend of the bench."

It looked as though Soapy was right. Nelson started the stars and played them for three full quarters. They didn't look bad! Finley got away for two long gains, but the freshman attack was confined to the ground, and the varsity used a 6-3-2 defense to hold it in check. The varsity attack wasn't much better but was versatile enough to score twice in the first half and again just at the end of the third quarter.

FRESHMAN QUARTERBACK

As the teams changed goals, Nelson electrified the despondent reserves on the bench by sending in a whole new team. English was at center, Montague and Waldorf at the guards, Cohen and Powell at the tackles, Smith and Schwartz at the ends, and Chip at quarter. Wells was at fullback, and Morris and Anderson took the halves.

The kickoff was short and low, and Chip pulled it in at full speed, veering to the left behind Schwartz and Cohen. His teammates dumped the two outside men, and Chip was away and racing to the varsity forty-five before he was knocked off his feet. He passed to Soapy for a first down on the thirty, sent Morris spinning over tackle for six, then faked a pass and dashed straight up the middle for a first down on the fifteen-yard line.

Chip had his teammates out of the huddle and over the ball before the varsity captain could call time. Chip then faked a lob pass to Soapy and lateraled to Morris, dashing far to the right behind the line of scrimmage. Speed scored standing up, and Chip kicked the point after touchdown.

Nelson and Sullivan were standing in front of the freshman bench, and the smiles they exchanged were far more expressive than mere words. Behind them, the stars sat mute and sullen. Nelson unexpectedly sent them in for the kickoff. It was a short kick, and an aroused varsity carried the ball all the way to midfield. A minute later they were knocking at the door with a first down on the freshman ten. Nelson called time then and turned to the bench.

"Come on, Hilton! Get your guys in there and show those prima donnas how to fight!"

Chip didn't wait for the others. He was on his way, pulling on his helmet as he ran. The huddle formed around him right under the crossbar. "Come on," he cried. "This is our chance to show we can play a little defense! We'll use a 6-3-2. Speed, you play back with me. Let's go!"

The last ten yards to the goal are always the hardest against a fighting, back-to-the-wall team. And that's what Chip's team was, a snarling, fierce group of scrappy underdogs formed in what practically amounted to a nine-man line. Smarting from the slights they had received, banded together by a common cause, the reserves were determined to prove they were as good as the stars and even better!

The varsity was confident but soon found out what sheer fighting spirit can do. They hit left tackle twice for no gain and then made the grave mistake of running the next play to Cohen's side. Biggie charged toward the ball, carrying the end and blocking back with him like two large stuffed animals from a carnival before smashing them head-on into the surprised runner for a three-yard loss.

It was fourth and thirteen, and Chip held the freshmen in the huddle until the last instant. Then he sent them into a 5-3-3 defense for the expected pass. Just as he'd figured, it was a toss into the end zone, which Speed Morris grabbed away from the expectant varsity receiver's hands for an interception. The freshmen took over on the twenty. Chip called a pass-action play right off the bat. Protected by the band of retreating linemen, he delayed as long as possible and then selected his receiver.

Chip's target was the freshman speeding down the right sideline without a backward glance, his mouthpiece jangling back and forth against his helmet. The blond quarterback aimed far ahead of the speedster and let the ball fly. An instant later he was buried under the charging varsity rushers. Chip and the blanket of varsity linemen were the only players on the field who didn't see Soapy Smith clutch the spiraling ball with straining finger tips on the varsity thirty-five. Soapy staggered and stumbled, but he held the ball and scored without ever looking back.

Soapy's teammates came whooping up the field and could scarcely be restrained until Chip converted the extra point. Their enthusiasm was irrepressible, the kind of spirit Curly Ralston had spoken about, that State spirit.

Coach Ralston signaled the end of the scrimmage before the freshman team could get set for another kick-off. Chip and his teammates headed to the showers on the run. The disgruntled and silent Booster stars followed slowly and sullenly.

As Chip and his four Valley Falls friends were leaving the field, they suddenly heard Petey Jackson yelling and saw John Schroeder and Doc Jones standing on the sideline waving to them. With a welcoming shout the boys headed for the little group and surrounded them, shaking hands and shouting wisecracks. They were pleased their hometown friends had seen the final minutes of the scrimmage.

"Hi ya, Soapy!" Petey yelled. "Smooth catch! Nice toss, Chip! Now hurry up, guys. I gotta get back to work!"

They were on their way thirty minutes later. Even so, they weren't the first to leave Camp Sundown. Practically everyone was in a hurry to get home for a well-deserved weekend. Two days didn't leave much time to spend at home and get back to college ready for the fall term.

But State's head coach was in no hurry. Ralston was plainly disappointed in his varsity. He walked slowly across the field, saying nothing. Henry Rockwell was fully sympathetic with Ralston's problem, but he was so thrilled by the play of Chip and the rest of his former Valley Falls stars that he thought it best to remain silent and wait for the head coach to speak.

"No kicker and no passer," Ralston muttered gloomily. "Can't go anywhere on the attack without a passer, and the defense is throttled without a kicker. I'm worried!"

"We'll turn up something, Coach," replied Rock confidently.

B. G. Anderson and his Booster friends were worried too. Their highly touted recruits had been shown up by a bunch of eager players they had never heard of, and they didn't like it. They headed for Nelson and Sullivan to plant a barb or two before consoling their discouraged athletes. Anderson, taking the lead, reached the freshman bench scarcely before the two coaches had time to pick up their clipboards and gear.

"What are you young coaches trying to do?" Anderson stormed. "Every time you scrimmage, you use the Booster players to wear out the varsity and then you put in the reserve no-names to get all the attention. What's the big idea?"

"We can't do it all ourselves," another Booster added. "You know these players have scholarships, and we put a lot of effort into keeping them happy. Remember, we're developing the future State varsity with these players, and they must play."

"That's right," a third Booster griped. "Why, they could check out right now and never play for State—now or in the future! Why don't you play it smart? Let them play. What do you have to lose? Don't you want to develop the best talent you have?"

"This isn't getting us anywhere," Anderson interrupted. "We'd better hurry down to the cabins and check on our players. Some of them are going straight back to the campus."

"How about taking them to lunch?"

"Good idea! We'll meet at Miller's."

"Where's Miller's?"

"Just before you reach Waterfield. Right where Route 19 crosses Route 20."

"OK. See you there!"

Anderson lagged behind for a last word with Nelson. "Why don't you cut those reserves?" he complained. "You've got enough Booster stars without them. From what I hear, a few of them are trouble waiting to happen."

Nelson shook his head stubbornly. "They aren't troublemakers, Mr. Anderson. But some of them are good football players. You saw what they did to the varsity."

"Let's not go down that road again. We don't need them on the freshman squad. They'll be around for next season's spring practice if they're any good and serious about football!"

"They *are* good! Right now! A few of them are good enough for the varsity. I just wouldn't feel right about cutting them. I do expect a few will drop out as the routine of dorm life, classes, practices, and studying gets to them. Besides, they're spread all over the campus in dorms while your Booster players live in Anderson House enjoying all that goes with it."

CHAPTER 5

Partings and Reunions

MARY HILTON, herself a tough tennis opponent and competitive golfer, had enjoyed sports all her life—first as a member of Valley Falls High School's varsity soccer and tennis teams, later as the sweetheart and wife of William "Big Chip" Hilton, star high school and college athlete, and then as the mom of "Little Chip," who had followed so surely in his father's footsteps.

Chip's mom had watched her son grow up and excel in football, basketball, and baseball—far beyond the hopes of his father. But Big Chip had never lived to see his son become the athlete of his dreams, and that had been the great tragedy in Mary Hilton's life, next to Big Chip's tragic death itself. All her struggles as a single mother to keep the little family going had been nothing compared to the loss of Big Chip in the prime of their life together.

It was a reunion at the Hilton home! Taps Browning, Chip's next door neighbor and a senior at Valley Falls, spent the afternoon looking out the window facing the Hilton house, anxiously waiting for his friend to get home. Suzy, his younger sister who was in her first year of high school, was almost as excited but for a different reason: she knew wherever Chip Hilton was, Soapy Smith would be close behind!

Taps and Suzy were the first to clamor up the Hilton front steps, but they were quickly joined by the entire crew. Chip's arrival filled the house with all the members of the Hilton Athletic Club. When Chip was a boy, his father had built a set of goalposts, a pair of baskets, and a pitcher's mound with a home plate in the backyard. Over the years, the Hilton A. C. had come to signify something even more meaningful than a place to play football, basketball, and baseball. Yes, the Hilton A. C. represented the close bond among Chip and his friends.

Hoops, Chip's long-haired cat, served as the unofficial welcoming committee by rubbing against each visitor and demanding to be stroked and petted over and over again. Chip's mom's gray eyes shone with the joy of having the house filled again with the good-natured joking and laughter that always prevailed when Chip's friends crowded into the family room. They ate slices of pizza, bowl after bowl of popcorn, and Soapy's all-time favorite, chocolate cake with chocolate icing.

Mr. and Mrs. Browning dropped in for a few minutes, too, and it was long after midnight before Hoops padded down the hallway to the door with the last departing guest for the final petting of the night. Then, for a little while, Chip and his mom were alone. There was a strong bond between mother and son, between the trim, athletic, middle-aged woman with light hair and gray eyes and the tall, handsome college freshman who resembled her so much. She knew the time Chip had just spent at student orientation and freshman football practice was only a taste of what lay ahead and that this last weekend before classes began would soon be over. But there would be other weekends to look forward to.

The atmosphere in the modest Hilton home in Valley Falls was a decided contrast to that in the luxurious residence of B. G. Anderson in University. Eddie and his father were alone in the impressive book-lined library, engaged in a bitter discussion.

"It just isn't fair," Eddie argued. "The best players are supposed to play. That's all there is to it!"

"The best players *are* playing," insisted his father.

"How can you say that? Chip Hilton isn't playing!"

"You think he's superior to Finley?"

"Chip Hilton is the best football player I ever saw!"

"Nonsense! He didn't show a thing until the varsity was worn down by the Booster stars."

"He didn't have a chance to show anything at the start. And even if he had started, the Booster clique would have tried to make him look bad."

"Son, you've been reading too many mystery stories or watching too many conspiracy movies at the mall. You make it sound like everyone in the university has a plot against this Hilton character."

"I'm not talking about fiction! I'm talking about what I see and hear. Every one of those stars you rave so much about ganged up on Chip, and he still looked good. That's more than you can say about your great Fireball Finley."

B. G. Anderson was frankly puzzled. After a brief silence, he said, "Eddie, why this sudden friendship with Chip Hilton? What's the matter with Finley? I'd hoped the two of you would become friends. *He's* going places!"

Eddie grunted disgustedly. "Sure," he agreed, "sure he's going places! In the showoff wheels you gave him and because you're his sponsor."

"The SUV wasn't given to him. It was only loaned to him."

"What's the difference? Anyway, how about me? *I* don't even have an old beat-up car to drive! This is my hometown! There's no rule against State students having cars if they live off campus."

"I've explained that to you time and again, son. Besides, don't you get to use one of our cars when you have a legitimate reason? It's the right decision, and I think you know it!"

"I don't know it! And I don't see how Fireball Finley's going to get away with it. Even if you *did* give it to him."

"Loaned!"

"Loaned then!"

A deep silence followed. Each was busy with his thoughts. Biz Anderson couldn't understand his son. He tried to give the boy all the things he had missed in his own youth: a college education, spending money, good clothes, and summer vacations. What more could a son want?

Eddie was thinking in the same vein. Why did fathers think all a guy wanted was good times, money, and pampering? Yes, that was the word. *Pampering!* Orchestrating everything he did, dissecting the parents of every girl he happened to date, trying to pick his friends . . . talk about being formatted! Come to think of it, that's all he was—computer software! And his father was the engineer and programmer! Did all the thinking and planning for both of them and then just downloaded it to him.

"Dad."

"Yes, Eddie?"

"Would you mind very much if I moved into one of the dorms and got a job?"

"Move into a dorm? Get a job? What in heaven's name for? What's the matter with this house? Why, it's the best house in town. And why in the world do you need a job? Don't tell me your spending allowance isn't ample! Are you wasting the money I give you? When I was your age, I had to scrape and work hard for every penny—"

"That's just it, Dad. I want to work too. Earn my own way, have my own money!"

"Nonsense! Playing football, studying, and keeping up your grades is enough of a job for anybody. How could you find time, even if I gave you permission to get a job?"

"Other guys find the time. Chip Hilton's going to work."

"So that's it! What in the world does this Hilton boy mean to you? Why can't you make friends with Finley and Pines and Maxim? Eddie, I just don't understand you at all! My word, is it seven o'clock? I've got to run! See you in the morning."

At the door, his father turned. "I wish you'd slip over to Anderson House and see if the players need anything, Eddie. Some of them couldn't go home this weekend. Too far to travel. And I said I'd look in on them. Good night, son."

Eddie grabbed the remote and punched on the wide-screen TV, but he didn't pay much attention to the ball-game. He was wrestling with a personal problem that seemed to have no answer. After a restless half-hour, Eddie set out for the freshman Booster house. He decided to give it another chance, try his best to warm up to the Booster stars.

State's Booster Association owned two houses in the town of University. One was under a long-term lease to a fraternity house, and the other was the new home for the freshman Booster stars. Both houses were situated on State University's campus in the most desirable location. In the earlier days at State, the houses had been faculty residences. Now, both had had their exteriors painstakingly refurbished and their interiors remodeled, offering all the comforts of home.

Eddie's pace slowed as he neared Anderson House, but when he reached the elegant oak porch, he pushed resolutely through the double doors and entered without knocking. He knew the surroundings well; he had been a frequent visitor in his high school days during the renovations and he knew where he would find the occupants.

Sean Reynolds called out to him, "Hey, Anderson, come on in. Have a seat."

Pete Pines, Lonnie Akins, Joe Maxim, and Bebop Leopoulos were all sitting around listening to one of Bebop's jazz CDs by Charlie "Bird" Parker. They greeted Eddie warmly, and Anderson's spirits rose. But then the quizzing began.

"This town's dead, Eddie. What's up?"

"Where's everybody hang?"

"They close up at sundown?"

"I'm hungry. Let's cruise for some food."

"Yeah. How about a ride around town? Show us the hot spots, Eddie. You got a car?"

Eddie grinned. "No. Wish I did. I'll be glad to show you around though."

"You mean walk?"

"No way! Fireball Finley rides, so we ride too!"

"You can say that again! Hey, Anderson! How come Finley gets a ride from your old man, and you haven't got one?"

Anderson shrugged. "Oh, I guess I could have one if I really wanted it."

"You mean you don't *really* want a machine like that?"

"Oh, I can't say that, but—"

"But what?"

"Well, I don't need it for one thing."

Sean Reynolds grinned broadly. "How about Finley? You think *he* needs a *sport utility vehicle?*"

Anderson was sweating now. He knew he was being grilled. Hard as it was, he tried to be friendly and answered all their questions as best he could. But he was glad when, at last, he said good night. Before he reached the sidewalk he heard a great burst of laughter and knew for certain that he would never fit in with that group of wisecracking, spoiled football stars. As much as he wanted to please his father, he decided right then the pressure of studies and football practice was going to limit the amount of time he would be able to spend at Anderson House.

All too soon, church was over and it was Sunday afternoon in Valley Falls. Slamming the trunk lid closed, Chip sighed and turned for one last look. The branches of the strong oak tree extended gracefully across the front of the small, white colonial house and cast cool shadows in the heat of the late summer sun. As always, Hoops lay preening himself, carelessly lounging in one of the two old wicker chairs on the front porch as if today were just any old day.

Chip's thoughts flew back, remembering a lifetime in this house, the only place he'd ever thought of as home. He'd learned how to ride his bike on this very sidewalk, how to steady himself over the bumps in the concrete and the spots where the spring grass popped through the cracks. When he was six, he and Speed first scaled the old oak, which wasn't quite so large or impressive back then but still loomed dangerously, a monumental challenge in two little boys' lives and a seal of their friendship.

And the Hilton A. C. in the backyard, lovingly constructed by his Dad, where he'd first fielded a ball and grew to know the father he'd loved so much for so short a time.

And the interior rooms of the house where the listening, warmth, prayers, laughter, and tears built the foundations of his life and sustained him through his father's death and the trials he and his mom had faced ever since.

"Almost ready, honey? Got everything?" Mary Hilton's voice floated from the porch, recalling Chip to the present.

"Yep! All ready, Mom. Now I'm glad I took most of my stuff at orientation."

Beep! Beep! Toot! Toot! A parade of five cars, horns honking, wound down Beech Street and pulled up in front of the Hilton home.

Outfitted in his red-and-blue State U. sweatshirt and blue State U. Bermuda walking shorts, an excited Soapy Smith whipped off his State U. baseball cap and jumped out of the lead car even before his father had rolled to a full stop.

"Chip, you ready yet? We're State-bound! We're college men! Let's get this caravan on the interstate! We're burning daylight!"

Speed leaned out the window and chuckled. "Hey Soapy, unique outfit. Show everyone your official State U. boxers!"

Without hesitating, Soapy unbuckled his belt, pulled down his Bermudas, and proudly posed in his official red-and-blue striped State University boxer shorts. Mr. Smith, seated behind the wheel, could only shake his head and retort, "Come on, Mr. College, or I'm dropping you and your boxers off at the bus station."

And they were off . . .

The caravan of five cars pulling out of Valley Falls probably looked the same as it had when the boys had left for orientation and football practice. Only this time, each carried a young adult who was becoming aware of a vast emptiness in his heart. Each felt unexpected loneliness that he had never experienced before. Sure, they'd all been away from home before on sports trips and at summer camps, even for long periods, but this time their going had a feeling of finality.

Chip was feeling proud of his mom, proud that she was a fighter. And he was proud of her gallant efforts, despite his constant protests, to make it possible for him to go to college. Chip was deeply aware of her many sacrifices for him. Now, as he sat next to his mom, Chip felt he was deserting her and leaving her to make the fight alone. He had wanted to go to work in Valley Falls, to support her and be responsible for the Hilton household. But Mary Hilton had persisted in her efforts, and now the long-awaited moment had arrived—Chip was on his way to college. Now it was up to him!

Soapy had been quiet, but the thrill of the big adventure of college gradually overcame the pangs of parting, and he was soon back in form. "Dad, when do we eat?"

"Didn't you have breakfast and lunch before we left?"

"That was hours ago. Besides, you know I always eat when we travel." Soapy's appetite managed to stretch a two-hour trip to three hours.

As they reached University, Chip's heart beat fast and hard. The streets were broad now, the stately red-brick classroom buildings separated from the sidewalks by deep, well-kept lawns. Tall and majestic maple, elm, and oak trees sheltered the buildings and lined the walks. Here and there, an ivy-covered stone or brick house caught the eye with a modest Greek-lettered sign in the front lawn or over the door, indicating a fraternity or sorority house. Students carrying backpacks zipped past on their bikes, following the bike trails running along the street and snaking between dorms and classroom buildings.

All the Valley Falls parents had visited State University before. But never had they been so deeply conscious of its impressive grandeur. Mrs. Smith described it best. "Why, it's like a big park! It's beautiful!"

The university buildings, which sat far back from the broad street, were framed by what seemed to be a forest of trees, alternating with beds of ancient laurel, rhododendron, and boxwood. Broad, shrubbery-bordered walks and paved drives seemed to lead in all directions, a perfect maze to the uninitiated.

Then they were pulling up in front of Chip's dorm, Jefferson Hall, a four-story, red-brick building setting some distance back from the street. "Jeff" was imposing. All the windows were the same size and distance apart, and there seemed to be a hundred of them. Well, there ought to be plenty of light for studying, Chip thought grimly as he surveyed the building and pulled his duffel bag from the back seat of the car.

"Now, you'll E-mail me as soon as you get your account set up, right?" Mary Hilton smiled and asked for the third time that afternoon.

"You know I will, Mom. I love you. Thanks for everything you've done," Chip replied as he squeezed his mom in a tender bear hug.

The five Valley Falls friends huddled together on the walk in front of their new home, watching their families depart. Chip, his hand raised in a salute as much as a farewell, watched as his mom's car, followed by the rest of the caravan, wove through the traffic on University Boulevard and disappeared around the bend. No one spoke until they had passed from sight.

"Hey, where's all the women?" Soapy demanded to break the tension. "I haven't seen even one coed!"

"They heard *you* were coming," Biggie growled, and the moment passed. Things were back to normal. College was going to be just fine. The group lugged the last of their things up the walk and were just about to swing through the double doors when a voice turned them around.

"Hey, wait up!" yelled Eddie Anderson.

"Hey, Eddie! What are you doin' here? You helping somebody move in, or you running away from home?" Soapy quipped.

"That's not a bad idea. Look, I've got more company."

Kip Waldorf and Dave English stood right behind him, grinning widely.

Anderson laughed. "Kip and Dave were switched to Jefferson Hall. You guys mind?"

"More the merrier," Biggie shrugged. "We're on the second floor. Let's go!"

The group rushed through the doors, Soapy sprinting for the elevator while everyone else took the stairs two or three at a time, arriving on the second floor before the elevator doors opened on a grinning, sheepish Soapy. The second-floor hall was filled with groups of newcomers like themselves, and Chip surveyed them carefully. These were the guys who would be his friends during his important freshman year, guys with whom he'd study, debate, work, philosophize, and dream of the future. They were a motley crew, some dressed in slacks and sports coats, some in shorts or sweats, but most in jeans and T-shirts. They came in all sizes and shapes, and from the mass congregated in the center of the hall emerged a broad-shouldered giant. He suddenly erupted into motion and barged through the crowd.

"Hey, you guys! Chip!"

The Valley Falls crew knew that voice! They were happy to see Joel Ohlsen, and even as they tugged and pulled at him, they were aware of the change. This wasn't the old Joel Ohlsen, the loud-mouthed, arrogant showoff they had known. His stint at military school had done a lot for the son of Valley Falls's wealthiest family. Gone were his flab, his sloppiness, his cocky attitude. This was almost a stranger, almost another Biggie Cohen for size and quiet assurance. But there was more. Some intangible inner quality was plainly visible in Joel's eyes and in the quiet control of his voice. And it all added up to the kind of person they wanted for a friend.

"How you been?"

"When did you get in?"

A hundred questions and answers were exchanged. Ohlsen's dad had driven Joel to school early that morning, and he was going to major in engineering.

"Ceramics?" Speed asked.

Joel grinned. "No, electrical engineering. What about you, Chip? Are you still thinking about the pottery business like our dads?"

Chip nodded. "I'm heading for all the science I can get."

"Me, I hate the stuff," Soapy complained. "And what happens? I end up with biology! Hah! Dead cats, frogs, ugh!"

"Well, Soapy, freshmen don't get a whole lot of choice," Eddie reminded him. "We've all got to take those basic requirements whether we want to or not."

PARTINGS AND REUNIONS

"Come on, guys, forget the gab and let's get into our rooms and finally get unpacked! We've got classes and practice tomorrow," Speed reminded them.

Chip and Soapy were roommates, and Biggie and Red Schwartz were right next door. Kip Waldorf and Dave English were just across the hall from Chip and Soapy. But the prize went to Speed and Joel, who had really lucked out, landing the biggest room on the floor at the end of the hall.

Chip opened the door to room 212, expelled a deep breath, shook his head, and slowly entered. Although he and Soapy had slept in their room during orientation and the first several football practices on campus, they had barely unpacked. Trunks, books, two computers, Chip's stereo, Soapy's TV, various posters, assorted boxes, and several suitcases were stacked to overflowing in every corner of the room. But there was something else. Perched on the pillow of Soapy's bed was a red and blue beanie with an attached letter that began, *"Dear Freshman, . . ."*

Soapy stormed on in, surveyed the mess, and wailed, "And where's the women?"

Eddie Anderson, standing just outside the door, responded, "Unless you scared them away, there's plenty around, Soapy."

Soapy immediately brightened. "You mean there's a million babes here?"

"Probably more. You'll see them at dinner."

"Eats!" Soapy yelled. "That's what's wrong! I'm starved! Soapy needs food!"

CHAPTER 6

Pulling the Chain

RED SCHWARTZ winked at Biggie Cohen and resumed the conversation. "That's the only way you can eat, Soapy," he said resignedly.

"You mean through the student union?" Biggie demanded, pretending amazement.

"That's right!"

Soapy listened to the conversation in astonishment. He decided to take a stand. "Well, I'm not joining any union," he announced defiantly.

"You still have to go to the student union," Red remarked calmly.

"That is, if you want to eat," added Joel.

"I refuse! I'll starve first!" Soapy retorted indignantly. "I never read anything in the orientation handbook about this! Just wait until I find that guy who took us around on the orientation tour!"

"Soapy, it's no big deal. I had to join the union at the pottery when I worked there each summer," Biggie confided. The usually serious Cohen was enjoying himself immensely.

Speed chimed in, "What about the coeds, Red?" he asked. "They have to go to the union too?"

"Sure do. Every one of them," Schwartz solemnly assured them while looking directly at Soapy. "They've all got to go to the union."

Soapy stopped short. "Really?" he managed. He thought it over briefly. "Well, maybe it isn't such a bad idea after all," he said hopefully.

The student union complex was one of the most modern in the country. The sprawling building extended in several directions, the wings housing restaurants, cafeterias, libraries, bowling alleys, student lounges, a few shops, and even a small hotel for campus speakers and guests. It was the best in student centers and the focal point of State's campus.

Soapy walked warily, his eyes darting in every direction. Then he saw the girls.

Eddie Anderson had been right! There were hundreds of them. Soapy straightened his shoulders and began his familiar swagger. "Where do we join the union? How much is it? Hope I can cover it," he jabbered eagerly.

Somehow, Soapy did not appreciate the roaring burst of laughter from his six friends. He scanned all of them, one at a time, trying to fathom the cause of their sudden amusement. Anderson eventually broke the news to him that they had been tugging his chain all along, that the student union was nothing more than a center for all students and faculty, a place where they might eat, read, bowl, hold meetings, stage their plays and debates, or just hang out.

Soapy was too deeply impressed for anger. As a matter of fact, he didn't think to get mad until after they had eaten and were on their way back to the dorm. Then he grabbed and roughhoused Schwartz down onto the library lawn. "You tricked me! Almost made me give up food! Never do that again!"

Two boys were sitting on the dorm's small porch when they reached Jeff. The smaller of the two walked toward Chip with eager steps. "Hey, Chip!" he called.

Chip grasped the friendly hand quickly. "Tug, how are you?" he said, shaking his old teammate's hand vigorously. "I didn't know you were at State! You going out for football?"

Tug Rankin's face sobered. "Not me, Chip, I've got a job. Won't have time to do much except study and work. By the way, here's an old rival of ours. Curt Warner! Hampton! Remember?"

"And how! Bull, how are you? Biggie, Speed, Joel, shake hands with Curt 'Bull' Warner. Soapy, Red, Eddie—Bull Warner, next to Tug Rankin, the best fullback in the state. How about that? Two fullbacks and neither one out for football! What's the idea, Bull?"

"Look at me," Warner chuckled, joining his hands in front of his stomach. "Look at the size of me." He laughed. "Nope, I like my eats!"

"Hey, you know something?" Soapy interrupted. "We've got a good football team right here."

"Too bad you guys can't play for Jeff," Anderson said. "You'd be a lock to win the championship."

"Why can't we?"

"Freshman and varsity players aren't allowed."

"No football for me," Ohlsen said quickly. "I've played enough! I'm up here for business!"

"I'd love to play," Tug Rankin said wistfully, "but I've gotta help pay my way here, and that means I've got to work. Dad's been scrimping long enough to keep me in school. I've got to get out and rustle my own way for a change. Anyway, I've got a job."

"The dorm teams don't practice much, even though they do take it seriously," Anderson said. "Why don't you play for Jeff? It's a lot of fun. Besides, I hear the championship dorm team will play the freshman team this year. Of course, the dorm champs won't compare, but they'll have lots of support."

"How come?"

"It's dorm life. Most students on the campus live in the dorms and turn out for games, contests, and parties."

Tug Rankin and Bull Warner managed to switch roommates and were assigned to a room on the third floor. It seemed like home to the Valley Falls crew, which spent the rest of the evening in Chip and Soapy's room, talking over old times.

Eddie Anderson listened quietly to the conversations, enjoying the close comradeship of the happy group, and he felt perfectly at home. After a while, he slipped away and started for Anderson House. He would have preferred to remain at Jeff Hall the rest of the night with the Jeff crowd, but he knew his father would ask if he'd seen any of the Booster stars, and he decided to avoid an argument.

An hour later he was on his way home, his face flushed with anger. He had made his last stop at the Booster house, had subjected himself for the last time to the constant ridicule. Eddie knew that behind it all was a subtle contempt for his father. Contempt for the very man who was making it possible for them to enjoy an education, meals, housing, and, Eddie reflected, goodness knows what else.

Eddie was right. He had been given a thorough initiation to being dissed, and it didn't end after his departure.

"That guy's as good as money in the bank to us!" Reynolds said. "We gotta make the most of him!"

"Stay away from his old man," Finley warned. "He's my project, and I don't want any competition."

Pete Pines chuckled. "We noticed!"

"You know, Fireball," Gilmore warned, "freshman students in the dorms aren't allowed to have cars on campus."

Finley laughed. "You said students," he chided. Then he became more serious. "I know, Bo, but I can get around that easily enough. There's more than one way to skin a cat."

"How's that?"

"Well, I'm not going to drive it on the campus, and it's being stored in Mulville, and that's five miles away."

"Yes, but—"

"No buts! I guess Anderson knows the rules! He said it would be OK. He told me this way I wouldn't be violating any rules."

"We're violatin' rules right now," Joe Maxim said significantly, nodding toward the clock. "Training rules! Let's hit the rack."

College students always seem to wait until the last day to get ready for the year's work. True to form, State's campus began to hum the following day. Eddie Anderson showed up early to take Chip and Soapy to see Mr. George Grayson. An hour later Chip Hilton and Soapy Smith were the newest employees at Grayson's. Anderson met them outside the door.

"We're in, Eddie," Chip exclaimed happily. "And it's all thanks to you. We'll be able to cover our expenses and have a little left over, and we won't have to cut into our funds for next semester's tuition. What a deal!"

Soapy was even more appreciative. He clapped Anderson on the back, threw his arms around the embarrassed freshman, and comically smooched him on the forehead.

"Wow!" Soapy yelled. "This almost makes up for your student union trick on me. Will my parents be surprised! Eddie, you're an angel or whatever football players are called up in heaven. Wow! I was sure worried about my meal plan. I didn't know how I was going to be able to afford three shakes a day."

"Three!" Chip echoed. "You mean six! Mr. Grayson doesn't realize it, but he's just hired a human sponge!"

"Aw, Chip," Soapy said in pretended humility, "I never call you names."

"What are your hours?"

"They're great, Eddie," Chip said. "Seven to eleven, Monday through Friday. It's perfect. We can play football, and well, it's just too good to be true. We start tonight."

Just then a well-dressed girl brushed past them and entered the store. Soapy's head swiveled around as if pulled by a string. "Wow!" he said breathlessly. "Wow! Who was that?"

"Mitzi Savrill," Anderson said quickly. "You'll see a lot of her. She's the head cashier."

Soapy gasped. "No!" he managed. "No! Be still my beating heart!"

"Yes!" Anderson laughed. "Five feet two, eyes of blue, and dynamite! Come on you guys, quit staring! There's a student government meeting in front of the union."

The meeting was already underway when they arrived. Student speakers were standing on a small platform on the commons, and it seemed the majority of State's twelve thousand students was there. Although it was old stuff to the upperclassmen, they were silent when the important freshman instructions were read by the student government officers.

In fact, there was scarcely a sound when the speaker announced that the freshman class elections would be held in the Student Union on Monday, October 10, at 11:00 A.M. and the election of dorm officers would take place in each dormitory on Friday, October 21, at 8:00 P.M.

At the end, the school pep band and varsity cheerleaders appeared, dressed in State's traditional red and blue with white trim. The freshmen really caught the State spirit, which they realized had their chests throbbing with school pride.

That same afternoon Jeff's freshmen held an informal meeting on the porch and discussed the rules they would have to observe through the first semester. Red Schwartz volunteered to read the rules if Soapy would assist him. Once again, Red yanked his friend Soapy's chain.

Schwartz mimicked the morning speaker as he ad-libbed the rules at Soapy's expense. "Freshman beanies must be worn at all times."

"What?" Soapy sneered. "They mean in bed too?"

"The freshman beanie must be lifted whenever an upperclassman of either gender is approached."

"I'll just turn my back," Soapy stated indignantly. "Only on the men, I mean."

"Freshmen must walk next to the curb on the sidewalk at all times."

Soapy snorted. "Do we have to wear a leash and bark like dogs?"

"Freshmen may not walk, ride, nor sit next to a member of the opposite gender in public."

Soapy howled. "Why don't they make us wear blindfolds too?"

"Freshmen may not occupy a place in front of an

upperclassman in any waiting line, particularly at the cafeteria."

"Now they want to starve us. I draw the line at this one. After all, I *am* a member of the student union," Soapy laughed.

"The final rule," Red announced with all sincerity, "Freshman Robert 'Soapy' Smith shall refrain from being so incredibly gullible, lest he give everyone a poor image of his upbringing and his hometown of Valley Falls."

Finally, Soapy caught on to Red's humor and chased him around the porch, over the rail, and off onto the lawn.

That's the way the next half-hour went, and Jeff's new residents thoroughly enjoyed it. It was the best way to break through the reserve that prevailed; Red and Soapy were just the ticket for the job.

After the real rules from the dorm adviser were read, the conversation swung to class schedules and the courses they were taking. Joel Ohlsen had missed the student government gathering because of an appointment with his adviser, and he attempted to explain to Soapy why certain freshman courses were required.

"But what if a guy doesn't want to be an engineer?" Soapy persisted. "What does he take?"

"The same thing."

"Why? I don't get it!"

"Well, the way Professor Holcomb explained it to me, every freshman takes certain required subjects so he'll have a foundation for specialization in his later years at the university."

"What if a guy wants to be a doctor?"

"Same thing."

"Bah! These guys up here don't know what they're doing!"

"Could be, Soapy," Cohen said dryly. "Why don't you tell them about it?"

Soapy swaggered defiantly. "I think I will! I think I'll start with Joel's adviser, that Holcomb guy. He doesn't seem too smart to me even if he is a phid."

"You mean a Ph.D."

"Ph.D. then. What's the difference?"

"Not much," Joel laughed, interrupting the treatment. "Believe it or not, Soapy's partly right. Phid is a contraction of Phidias, I seem to remember, at least it could be. Anyway, Ph.D. and Phidias are both related to advanced studies, postgraduate study, that is."

"So!" Soapy exploded. "But what's that make this Holcomb guy? Just what does this Ph.D. stuff really mean?"

"It means he's completed an intense course of studies and research in a special field and is regarded more less as an authority, a doctor, so to speak—doctor of philosophy, doctor of jurisprudence—"

Soapy was thoroughly mixed up now. "I never heard of anyone being sick with either one of those diseases," he said dubiously.

When the laughter subsided, Schwartz winked behind Soapy's back. "They say Dr. Holcomb's the greatest living authority on the diseases afflicting the common flea," Red said admiringly. "He studies them in action."

"No way!" Soapy cried.

"Yes!"

"Then how's he study the fleas in action?"

"The students."

"You mean the students gotta bring the fleas?"

"No, he provides them. All they got to do is wear them during class."

Soapy was horrified. "No way!"

PULLING THE CHAIN

Then he was struck by a horrible thought. Mumbling apprehensively, he suddenly dived into his pocket and pulled out his class schedule.

"What's this guy teach, this Dr. Holcomb?" he asked feverishly.

Red Schwartz nodded his head delightedly to the nearly hysterical audience. "Biology 101," he said, "section 17."

Soapy threw his card up in the air. "I'm going home!" he said dramatically. "It's been nice knowing you guys!"

That broke up the meeting. Chip hurried upstairs to shower and clean up for dinner. He wanted to look his best the first evening on the job at Grayson's. Soapy followed soon after, muttering about philosophy and doctors and phids and Ph.D.s and all the nonsense going to college involved when all a guy wanted to do was learn to earn a living.

"Me, I'm all mixed up," he complained to Chip. "I don't know whether I want to be an engineer or a doctor or a phid, I mean a Ph.D., or a pharmacist like Schroeder or a newspaper writer or a lawyer like Speed's dad or a sports announcer."

"That's the reason for the liberal arts courses for the first year or two, Soapy," Chip explained patiently. "Just as Joel was trying to tell you. It's sort of an orientation to lots of options before you have to choose your major."

Soapy stared at Chip admiringly. "That's more like it," he said enthusiastically. "This getting oriented stuff's right down my alley. I'm starting my orie—my orientat—my getting acquainted right now! Mitzi Savrill, here I come!"

CHAPTER 7

Local Yokel!
Local Yokel!

MITZI SAVRILL lifted her violet-blue eyes demurely and extended a small, cool hand to Chip. "I'm very happy to know you, Mr. Hilton," she said coyly in her southern accent. To Chip's utter confusion, she held tightly to his hand, seemingly unaware of everyone but him, completely absorbed. A wave of red swept clear to Chip's eyes as he gently pulled his hand away.

George Grayson grinned with amusement. The owner of Grayson's had seen Mitzi operate before. This tall, good-looking Hilton youngster was destined for quite an education.

"And this is Soapy Smith."

Mitzi turned reluctantly toward Soapy and nodded pleasantly. "It's a great pleasure to know you, Mr. Smith," she said, displaying small pearl-like teeth in a dazzling smile.

Soapy stood with his mouth open as if hypnotized but finally tore himself away from the fascination of Mitzi's eyes only because Chip elbowed him in the ribs, grabbed him by the arm, and half dragged him to follow Grayson toward a store counter. There they were introduced to Ken Woods and another State coed, Jane Adams. Soapy seemed to be in a trance, alarmingly quiet.

Two State students, wearing red-and-blue polo shirts and white pants, eyed them appraisingly as they approached the restored soda fountain counter.

"These are the new fellows I told you about," Grayson said pleasantly. "Chip Hilton and Soapy Smith. Shake hands with John Park and Alex Rodriguez. I'll leave you two now and let you get acquainted with our prices, the store, and your spots: the fountain and food areas. John and Alex will fix you up with the right work attire. Welcome aboard. See you later."

Fountain work was old stuff for Chip and Soapy. Park and Rodriguez appreciated how quickly the two new employees adapted themselves to their jobs and moved along to the food court. But this was no Sugar Bowl setup. There was no time for gossip or leisurely conversations on this job. The long row of stools in front of the fountain, the tables, and the booths were occupied, all the time. The students who waited on the tables and booths were stepping on each other's heels, it seemed, with their impatient orders for pizzas, burgers, fries, nachos, sandwiches, salads, hot-fudge sundaes, and banana splits.

Soapy, working furiously, concentrated on his job. But Chip noticed that every time a customer delayed a second longer than necessary to get change or was fortunate enough to draw a smile from Mitzi, Soapy started to grumble. Eleven o'clock came as a surprise. Chip was in a hurry to get back to his dorm room, but Soapy delayed long enough to see Mitzi leave with another girl. Then the guys headed for Jeff, walking along thoughtfully and quietly.

"Sounds like the name of an actress, doesn't it?"

Chip was startled. Soapy must have been reading his thoughts. "Why, er, yes, she—What did you say?"

Soapy peered at him suspiciously. "You heard me!" he said flatly.

Chip was up early the next morning, anxious to get to his first college class. He found the two-tiered classroom easily enough but checked the schedule twice to make sure he was in the right room. *Wow! All these students are in this class? There must be more than 150 students in here.* The bell rang.

Chip Hilton had started college.

English 101 quickly initiated Chip into the college lecture method. There were no discussion, no call for answers, no raising of hands. The professor lectured impersonally, pausing from time to time to remind the class of the importance of note taking. Just before the bell, she read a long list of titles for independent reading and passed out the course syllabus. "Very confidentially," she added in a precise voice, "I advise you to spend considerable time in the library if you wish to pursue this course satisfactorily. That is all for today."

Chip and Biggie reported early for football practice that afternoon and were amazed at the efficiency of the trainers and the equipment managers in handling the huge squad of varsity and freshman hopefuls. Several freshman newcomers, easily spotted because of their brand-new equipment, reported for the first time.

State boasted three athletic sites. Alumni Field was immense and open to all students and faculty of the university. It contained five playing fields, two for baseball or softball, two for soccer, and a football field surrounded by a six-lane, all-weather track. Each athletic field had seating for 750 to 1,000 spectators. In season, the football field was used exclusively for dorm intramural games and the new freshman football team.

University Stadium was a modern, horseshoe-shaped, multilevel facility. The rich green playing field was accented by a ten-lane, red-colored, all-weather track. The varsity football practice fields were just outside the closed end of the stadium, and the weight training rooms were on the lower level next to the team locker room. University Stadium seated nearly sixty thousand spectators and was restricted to varsity seasonal events such as football games, soccer matches, and track meets, as well as the annual commencement exercises. Next to the stadium complex was Assembly Hall, which held the offices of the athletic administrators and their staffs, the coaching offices, and the fifteen-thousand-seat basketball facility.

There must have been a hundred players running and passing and kicking on Alumni Field when Chip and Biggie checked in. Most of these were dorm players practicing in groups at the far end of the field until the freshman practice began. One by one, the freshman candidates turned up and aligned themselves. The Booster stars surrounded Finley near one goal, while Chip was the focal point for the reserves.

Nelson's shrill whistle brought them together in the big circle where practice always started with Sullivan's famous grass drill.

"Circle out!" the big line coach called. "Circle out and get those arms up! Give yourselves enough room! All right now. Heads up! Stay alert.

"In place, mark time! Standing run! Let's lift those knees now! Lift 'em high. Hit that old chin! On the count, ready? 1-2-3-4-5-6-7-8-9 and 10. Speed it up now! 1-2-3-4-5-6-7-8-9 and 10. On the double now! 1-2-3-4-5-6-7-8-9 and 10! Stop! On your backs, in place! Bicycle! Get those legs up. Let's see them churn. On the count! Let 'em go! Steady, stop!

"On your feet! On your back! On your stomach! Up, up on your feet! Down, down on your hands and knees! In place now, push-ups: 1-2-3-4-5-6-7-8-9 and 10. Stop! Sit-ups now! 1-2-3-4-5-6-7-8-9 and 10. Stop!

"On your back. Ready! Head and feet, now. Arch it up! Ready! Down! Up! Down! Up! Down! Up! Steady, halt! On your belly! Push up! On the count! Ready: 1-2-3-4-5-6-7—Hold it everybody!"

Sullivan's face was livid with anger as he strode over in front of Pete Pines. "Look, Pines," he bellowed, "If you don't want to put out, get out! You hear? You've been sluggish since the first day we hit camp. Put out or get out! Understand?" He turned and stalked back to the center of the circle. Then he placed his hands on his hips and delivered an ultimatum to the entire squad.

"That goes for the rest of you so-called players who've been dogging it too! You know who you are! So do we! I'm sick and tired of looking at a few wimps who don't want to work! Football's a game of condition, and it's my job to get you in shape. So you're going to get in shape or get out!

"All right, Nik, you take 'em. I'm sick of looking at some of these so-called wonder boys! Hah! Wonder boys!"

Nelson took over and separated the squad into two teams and scrimmaged the entire session. There weren't any touchdowns. One team would take the ball and run a play, and the other team would try to break it up. Then the second team would take the ball and run a play, and the first team would try to stop it. Whenever a runner broke away, the whistle would check him, and they would do it all over again until the defensive team stopped the play cold. It was a killing practice.

Chip and his group were once again with the reserves, and they gave the Booster stars more than they could handle. Chip broke away almost every time he ran over Cohen's tackle position, and his passes clicked regularly whenever Soapy and Red were at the end positions. During a particular pass series, Chip's passes clicked seven straight times against the stars. Nelson really blew his top then, spewing all over Finley, McGuire, Rentler, and Roberts.

"You guys ever play pass defense? Can you spell pass defense?" Nik demanded angrily. "Maybe you ought to bring your clippings to practice someday and show us how you used to play football. Oh, excuse me! You're stars! I forgot that! You're not supposed to play defense! You don't get your name in the papers that way! Hah!

"OK, Hilton! You keep right on throwing that ball. They'll learn pass defense if we have to stay here all night!"

The freshmen did just about that. Nelson kept them until 6:30. That was one evening Chip and Soapy didn't relax in the showers. They were in and out and gone. They arrived at Grayson's just under the wire at 6:55.

Back in the freshman dressing room, the Booster stars were complaining, sullenly rebellious.

"How'd Sullivan get that way?" Pines demanded. "Wait'll I let that Booster guy, Thomas, know what's going on—"

"Aw, shut up!" Finley said in disgust. "If you guys keep on playing around, you're going to run into some real trouble."

"You should talk," Bebop retorted. "What makes you think you're the only guy who wants to play football?"

"I didn't say that."

"Sure!" Akins interrupted. "Why should you? Why should the great Fireball Finley complain? Didn't one of the local yokels come through with a full ride at State and a car and an allowance and—"

"All right," Finley retorted angrily, "so what? What's that got to do with you?"

"Nothing, except the rest of us wouldn't mind having one of those local yokels ourselves."

"What do you expect me to do, put an ad in the paper for you? Look, I'm doing all right. You guys get out and work on your own meal ticket. Go get your own local yokel."

Two rows away, sitting dejectedly on the narrow bench behind the lockers, Eddie Anderson listened to the conversation, trembling with rage and feeling complete helplessness. His first impulse had been to tear around the lockers, grab the first one he saw, and tell the whole bunch off. But he was intelligent enough to realize that a fight couldn't possibly help.

So Eddie Anderson sat there and took it, took it with a discouraged heart and a resentment that found expression only in clenched fists and a determination to even the score some way with this unappreciative crew. And especially with Fireball Finley!

Chip and Soapy were too busy to think about football the rest of that evening, but freshman football buzzed in several other minds. Nelson and Sullivan sat in their office long after showering with no thought of food.

"I just couldn't take it any longer," Sullivan exploded irritably. "Every time I look at that sniveling Pines and the rest of those prima donna Booster stars, I burn."

"*You* burn?" Nelson interrupted. "How do you think I feel? How much longer are we going to be able to stand this?"

LOCAL YOKEL! LOCAL YOKEL!

Ironically, that same question was being voiced at about the same time in Anderson House. Pete Pines was still denouncing Sullivan and loudly broadcasting the letter he was going to write to his local yokel, Hunk Thomas.

"Thomas will take that Sullivan apart," he fumed. "Wait until he gets my letter! What's that big beanhead want me to do? Play on a broken ankle?"

"Now, Pete," Finley chided, "you know it isn't that bad. You've been coasting. Taking it easy for ten days on a little sprain."

"Sprain! Man, I couldn't walk!"

"You always managed to get to the head of the cafeteria line."

"So what? I'm in shape now! What's the big dork want?"

"I know what I want," Akins growled. "I want a good crack at that grandstander. That Hilton!"

"Make that two of us," Leopoulos added.

"You hear Nelson patting him on the back this afternoon?" Sean Reynolds asked sarcastically. "Anyone can stand back there and throw a ball."

"Not like that guy throws them," Finley dissented. "Hilton throws a football as easily as I throw a rock."

"Aw, that pass stuff is nothing," Akins grumbled. "Football's a running game."

"You hear what that jerk Nelson said?" Pines asked bitterly. "What's he all about?"

Finley laughed shortly. "Same thing that was troubling Sullivan," he said. "Nelson thinks we haven't been working! And you know something? We haven't! We've been acting like we own those two guys." Fireball stood up and stretched his arms above his head. "Well, I'm out of here. Excuse me, freshmen, but I'm going to do a little studying."

"You mean you can't study here?" Pines demanded.

"I like atmosphere, and this isn't it."

"Yeah, right," Akins said knowingly. "And remember, no vehicles on campus!"

"Yeah," Leopoulos added. "But studying with an open sunroof by moonlight and the CD player pouring out the 'Bird' or Dizzy Gillespie is mellow on the ears. There's nothing like jazz! That's why everybody calls me Bebop."

"Hey!" Reynolds shouted. "You forgot your books!"

Finley didn't hear that last jab. He was off, heading for State and Tenth and concentrating on a very important subject. Something he had discovered at Grayson's that he figured would require constant attention and deep concentration.

B. G. Anderson was at peace with the world that evening. He sat in the cherry-paneled library, an open book in his lap, and reviewed the day. All of the football stars on the Booster roster had attended their classes. He sighed contentedly and reached for his pipe. Eddie would be along any minute now, and he'd learn how practice had gone that afternoon.

Anderson was a wealthy man. He could have retired from all business activity years earlier. But he was energetic, and he loved to meet a challenge with a good fight. And he loved publicity. Stepping in to support State's freshman pilot program had given him the chance to receive the adulation and attention he craved. He had been so enthusiastic and so lavish with his donations to the Booster athletic fund that he soon found himself in the driver's seat, the big wheel in the operation of the policies of State's Booster Association.

Anderson was the type of man who attempted to dominate every person with whom he came in contact. In all his undertakings, he had to take the reins in hand.

LOCAL YOKEL! LOCAL YOKEL!

Besides, the new head coach, Curly Ralston, was too involved with the varsity and had played no part in bringing these new players to State. So it was up to him. But he wasn't satisfied with just backing the incoming freshman players the former head coach had recruited. He wanted to supervise the coaching and second-guess the decisions of the freshman staff. He assured himself constantly that he had gotten into this athletic business just to encourage his son, and he couldn't understand why Eddie didn't appreciate his dedicated effort.

Eddie Anderson fumed all the way home. Why was his father so blind? Eddie took the broad steps three at a time and barged into the house, at odds with everything and everyone.

The irritating slam of the front door interrupted B. G. Anderson's thoughts. "Eddie," he called, "come here."

"Yes, Dad?"

"I wish you wouldn't slam that door."

"Sorry, Dad. I wasn't thinking."

"How was practice?"

"It was different, well, a little different for a change."

"Why?"

"The coaches were fired up for one thing."

"What about?"

Eddie hesitated, torn between his desire to tell the truth about the stars and his reluctance to have an argument with his father. But the anger that had gripped him in the locker room returned, and the words streamed forth in a furious torrent.

"About the dogging it and conniving and all the things I've been trying to tell you about your precious wonder stars. They gave it to them good!"

"The criticism was directed solely toward the Booster players, I suppose."

"You got that right! And you want to know something else? Chip Hilton passed your Wonder Team silly—the line, the defensive backs, the safeties—all of them! He had Finley and Rentler and McGuire and the rest of those bozos tripping all over themselves!"

"I suppose Nelson had nothing but praise for this Chip Hilton."

"That's exactly right! Chip threw seven straight one time—"

"Chip?"

"Yes, Chip! He's the nicest guy I ever met! Why, he's so far superior to your wonder boy Finley it isn't even funny. Chip can run and pass and kick, and he's intelligent. Fireball Finley can't do a thing but run, and when it comes to brains—"

"That's enough, Eddie. I don't intend to listen to such nonsense any longer."

Eddie couldn't resist a parting shot. "Someday," he said bitterly, "you'll find out what Fireball Finley really thinks about you." He turned abruptly and left the room. And all the way upstairs to his room, Eddie's thumping feet beat out a perfect rhythm:

"Local yokel! Local yokel! Local yokel! Local yokel!"

CHAPTER 8

The Wonder Team

FIREBALL FINLEY strode swiftly and confidently after leaving Anderson House, but his pace slowed when he reached Main and Tenth. He glanced around and then sauntered over to Grayson's and pretended to examine the items in the front window's display case. A covert inspection beyond the window and toward the cashier's desk inside assured him his trip had not been in vain. He walked into the store and turned toward the old-fashioned soda fountain. Then he saw Chip and stopped short, completely caught off guard. One quick look at the red-and-blue polo shirt and white pants was all Fireball needed. He ambled over to the counter and sat down directly in front of Chip.

"Small world, isn't it?" Finley said. "What's up?"

Chip placed a glass of water and a napkin on the counter.

"I guess you could call it an extracurricular activity, Fireball. What'll you have?"

"Oh, gimme a burger and fries and a chocolate shake. Hey, Smith. You're here too?"

Soapy snorted. "Me? *Why Mr. Finley!* Don't you recognize an epicurean expert when you see one? You'll have to excuse me. I have to take care of one of my clients."

Finley smiled and leisurely attacked the chocolate shake. Wait until the guys at the Booster house hear about this! Maybe he ought to call them! No, that wouldn't do. They'd be down here in two seconds. And one look at the cashier and they'd never leave.

Finley sat and considered his next move while he leisurely ate his food. Then he picked up the check. "See you tomorrow, you guys," he said amiably.

Soapy was extremely busy, but he recognized the reason for the Booster star's sudden hunger pangs. So did Chip. And so did Mitzi Savrill!

Mitzi knew all about Fred "Fireball" Finley. In fact, the extent of Mitzi's knowledge about anything and everything connected to the university would have surprised most people. It didn't surprise her employer, George Grayson, but it did continue to amaze Howard Wendel, owner-editor of the *University Herald*. Few people knew that this intelligent little heartbreaker was the established columnist of "The Chattering Scribbler" column, which appeared six days a week under the nom de plume Birdie Byrd.

"Can I help you, Mr. Finley?"

Fireball was shocked. His mouth dropped open in surprise, and he gazed at Mitzi in disbelief. But it was only for a second. His quick wit came to the rescue, and he took advantage of the unexpected opportunity.

"How did you know my name?"

"Why, everyone knows about Mr. Firegall Finley, the greatest quarterback in the country," Mitzi drawled.

"That's Fire*ball*."

THE WONDER TEAM

"Oh, I thought it was gall!"

"No, it's ball, as in football. What's your name?"

"You mean you've been here since yesterday and don't know my name? Why, Mr. *Finally*—"

"Finley!"

"Oh, yes, Firegall Finley. Well, my name is Savrill. Mitzi Savrill."

Soapy's latest customer looked up in surprise when he found two scoops of ice cream in his Coke. He pointed to the glass and shrugged his shoulders when Soapy handed him a spoon. Soapy kept his left ear tuned in the direction of the cashier's desk, but he couldn't hear a word of the conversation. He looked at the clock and gloomily calculated that it had taken Fireball Finley less than two minutes to get into an extended conversation with Mitzi while he hadn't been able to say two words to her in exactly six hours and thirteen minutes!

The rest of that evening was tough for Soapy's customers. Orders were lost or mixed up, and complaints were met by Soapy's coldest glare. Most of the regulars passed off the mistakes to the new employee's inexperience.

Chip had his own troubles. There just weren't enough hours in the day. Classes, studying, football practice, and the new job left little free time. Busy as he was, he found time to sit at his computer and E-mail his mom every day. He told her all about his classes, professors, his adviser, Professor Hansen, and the new job at Grayson's. He even mentioned Soapy's interest in Mitzi Savrill. He hadn't known just how to tell his mom about the football trouble, but the Friday issue of *The Statesman*—the university's official undergraduate newspaper—solved that one. Several articles interested Chip. He decided to scan them and send them to his mom.

FRESHMAN QUARTERBACK

FRESHMAN CALENDAR

Mon. Oct. 10 Class Elections
Student Union, 11 AM
Fri. Oct. 21 Dorm Elections
Dorm Lounges, 8 PM

FRESHMAN GRIDIRON SQUAD
TABBED AS WONDER TEAM
by Gil Mack

Alumni and Booster football fans are holding their breath for the unveiling on Alumni Field of State's new freshman Wonder Team against Carleton Community College, at 10:30 Saturday morning, October 8.

The heralded stars are led by Fred "Fireball" Finley, the six-foot 210-pound sensation who was selected for the all-American high school eleven last season. The brilliant redhead has proved to be pure dynamite in the intrasquad scrimmages.

In high school, Finley was a T quarterback. The coaching staff plans to build the attack around the renowned star. Head Coach Nik Nelson has named the following freshmen for the starting slots on the offense:

Finley at quarterback; Mike McGuire and Ricky Rentler at the halves; Junior Roberts at fullback. McGuire is a hard-running back, stands five-eight and tips the scales at 170. Rentler, five-eleven, 195 pounds, is an outstanding blocker. Junior Roberts stands six-three and weighs 230. Roberts looks slow, but Nelson says he is one of the fastest backs on the squad.

THE WONDER TEAM

Stavros "Bebop" Leopoulos is an outstanding freshman center. The fast, aggressive Greek star is six-one, and a solid 190 pounds.

The guards stack up with Bo Gilmore, six feet, 205 pounds, and Lonnie Akins, six-one and 195 pounds; at the tackle spots, Bob Dean, six-one and 218, and Joe Maxim, six-two and 210.

The ends are manned by Sean Reynolds and Pete Pines. Both stand six feet and are lightweights compared to their teammates. Reynolds is 167, while Pines weighs in at 175.

Defensive coach Jim Sullivan was uncertain about the defensive opening-day lineup but named Anderson, Morris, Carson, and Hilton as possibilities for secondary assignments; Garcia, Schwartz, and Smith as linebackers; and Cohen, Montague, Wells, and Waldorf as outstanding contenders for line duty.

Coaches Nelson and Sullivan stated that it might be necessary for some of the starters on the offense to assume defensive responsibilities. But they would prefer to develop specialists as they sort through the numerous walk-on candidates and scholarship players.

Coach Curly Ralston, State University's new head coach, commented that this freshman squad is the result of State's new pilot program, instituted to provide incoming freshmen with a solid educational foundation and thereby increase graduation rates among all athletes. State's future football fortunes are decidedly on the upswing.

FRESHMAN FOOTBALL SCHEDULE

* Sat.	Oct. 8	Carleton Comm. College	Alumni Field
Sat.	Oct. 15	Midwestern Prep	Away
Sat.	Oct. 22	York Junior College	Away
Sat.	Oct. 29	Midland Junior College	Away
* Sat.	Nov. 5	Waynesburg Comm. College	Alumni Field
* Sat.	Nov. 12	Dorm Champions	Alumni Field
Sat.	Nov. 19	Oxford Comm. College	Univ. Field
* Thurs.	Nov. 24	A. & M. Freshmen	Alumni Field

*Morning Games

Chip sighed as he sent the E-mail document containing the clippings and a letter to his mom. He knew she would understand a lot of things after she read Gil Mack's freshman Wonder Team story.

Gil Mack, student sports editor, researched most of the material for his article from State's sports information director's office. A brief talk with Nik Nelson and Jim Sullivan by phone had resulted in the naming of the starting lineup, and Gil had permitted his imagination to fill in the rest of the story. He would have been amazed to know the frenzy the article was about to cause.

Students couldn't wait to get their copies of *The Statesman,* which came out each Friday afternoon. Eddie Anderson had just left his last class of the day, a two-hour lecture in biology, when he grabbed his copy on the way to the cafeteria. He was absorbed in his lunch until he ran across the freshman story. Then his appetite disappeared.

Before Eddie had even finished the article, he was filled with indignation at the injustice and didn't bother to finish his lunch. Pushing away his tray, he started for home. He waited there all afternoon, cutting football practice, impatiently pacing the floor until his father arrived.

B. G. Anderson scarcely had time to close the door before Eddie shoved *The Statesman* into his hands. "Read this!" Eddie said angrily.

"Well, let me get my jacket off," B. G. protested. "What's the rush? What's wrong with you?"

"Plenty! Just read this garbage about the freshman team."

"Garbage?"

"Yes, garbage! Cheap, useless, and nothing but garbage!"

Eddie followed his father into the library and remained standing while his dad settled himself in his favorite leather chair. "Now, let's see what this is all about."

When B. G. finished reading the story, he looked up questioningly. "I don't understand, Eddie. What do you mean?"

"It's garbage! I mean it's unfair. Chip Hilton and Biggie Cohen are the two best football players in the whole school, including the varsity. And they're hardly mentioned. It's *unbelievable!* It's ludicrous, that's what it is! Completely ludicrous!"

The argument was loud and futile, resulting in a stalemate. When he saw it was useless to continue, Eddie dejectedly headed upstairs to his room.

Remarkably, Chip was the only one of his friends who had read the story before practice that afternoon, and he said nothing. But when Joel Ohlsen found his roommate studying hard in their room later that evening, he pulled *The Statesman* from his backpack and angrily poked his finger at the sports page.

"You see this?" he asked significantly.

Speed Morris shook his head. "No, what?"

"Check it out!"

Minutes later Red Schwartz and Biggie Cohen responded to Speed's yell down the hallway to "come in here a minute" and got the bad news.

"What do you think of this?" Speed asked gloomily.

Biggie shrugged his massive shoulders. "No big deal. We expected it, didn't we?"

"I suppose so," Speed said heavily, "but it's really unfair to you and Chip."

Schwartz angrily banged his fist on Joel's desk. "You know what I think I should do?" he demanded. "I should tell Rock what's been going on!"

"No way, Red!" Biggie said decisively. "We'll fight our own battles. Look, we know Chip belongs on that team, and it doesn't require much strain on the brain to figure out why he isn't—"

"The answer's Fireball Finley!" Schwartz exploded angrily.

"Not entirely," Biggie countered. "Nelson and Sullivan have to play ball with Eddie's dad."

"And Anderson sponsors Finley!" Speed added.

Cohen nodded. "You got it."

"So?" Ohlsen queried. "What do we do?"

"Nothing, give it time," Biggie advised. "Chip will get a break. You'll see! He'll make his own breaks. In the meantime, don't say a word to him about this. Maybe he won't see a paper. Let's get rid of any *Statesman* lying around the dorm and keep him busy tomorrow. How's that?"

Chip had expected some caustic comments from his friends about the article when he and Soapy reached Jeff that night after work. He was surprised when no one even mentioned the story. His freshman buddies overplayed things a little though, and after Chip got off the Internet, he chuckled to himself. *Who do they think they're fooling?*

Saturday was no problem. The schedule was full, with football all day. Practice in the morning, a football parade at noon, the varsity game in the afternoon, and the football dance that night at the Student Union.

Nelson and Sullivan had dreaded the Saturday morning practice because they knew every member of the squad must have read the Wonder Team story. As they dressed, they commented briefly on the woes of sportswriters.

"They're all alike," Sullivan growled. "Anything for a story."

"I ought to write everything out and then hand it to them," Nelson said regretfully. "Then they couldn't twist my words around. No more phone interviews for me!"

"It's going to be rough on some of those kids, Nik. Especially Hilton and Cohen."

"Well, who'd ever think Gil Mack would write up the story that way?"

"Right! Nik, you think anybody will drop out?"

"Don't you believe it!" Nelson replied. "They know all about Anderson House, and the way they've been banging the stars around in the scrimmages is a pretty good indication of how they feel. No, the real ballplayers won't quit. Granted, we'll probably hear it from some of them! Come on. Let's get it over with."

The freshman coaches got a surprise. There wasn't the slightest evidence of sulking or griping or resentment among the reserve players. Chip and the rest of the Valley Falls players were focused on football. But the coaches knew that it would only take a spark for something to happen. The reserves needed only the leadership of Chip Hilton to initiate the action.

The Booster stars, feeling self-important, discharged a few sly innuendoes. Nelson took care of that. He literally ran the whole squad speechless. There wasn't much talk left in anyone when that practice session was over.

Later, the guys from Jeff followed the band to University Stadium. The area surrounding the vast sport complex was a madhouse. Fans and students moved restlessly in all directions, talking excitedly at their tailgate parties, shoving, pushing, laughing, and rushing breathlessly here and there. Actually, there was no need to hurry. It was early, long before game time.

The Jeff crowd was directed en masse to sections M and N. Down below, on the bright green grass, both teams were warming up. Chip was dazzled by the bright State colors, reds and blues everywhere he looked, and by the life and wonderful spirit gripping every football fan on this perfect autumn Saturday.

Across the field, the visitors were seated in sections D, E, and F, and below them, right behind the southeastern bench, their band was blaring away. Below Chip, the red-and-blue-uniformed State band, wearing red-plumed hats, alternated with their counterparts, playing spirited music. In the sections to the right and left, it seemed there were hundreds of happy couples. Most of the girls were wearing State colors, and many were waving State pennants. As Chip scanned the crowd, all the girls seemed to exude that "sporty" freshness and outdoor look that Soapy was always talking about.

Chip guessed that Mitzi Savrill was there, too, some-where—and probably with a good-looking guy wearing the latest name-brand fashion statement. Not that peo-ple would pay much attention to him or his outfit once they caught a glimpse of Mitzi. He knew it was silly, but he tried to find her in the crowd just the same. Then he laughed out loud at himself, remembering the evening when Mitzi had called over to him for a Coke. When he carried it over to her, she'd asked him if he liked to dance. He could still see her smile and hear her voice when she had said, "I'd rather hoped you did, Chip. I'd love to go to the football dance Saturday night." As Chip turned away, she had continued provocatively, "Are you *sure* you don't dance?"

Chip smiled again and then forgot all about the memory and Mitzi, too, as the teams lined up for the kickoff. There wasn't much to laugh about the rest of that afternoon. Curly Ralston must have suffered as much as anyone else as the Statesmen absorbed a 28-12 defeat.

Later, a subdued crowd gathered in Chip's room with no plans for the evening. Except for Soapy. He was dressed and determined to hit the dance. "How about it, Chip? Come on, you don't have to dance."

Chip laughed.

"You can watch, can't you?"

"All evening? No way! Not me!"

"How about a movie, and then we can drop in?"

Chip reluctantly agreed and eventually wound up outside the Student Union.

"There'll be a lot of babes here, Chipper," Soapy said happily. "Me, I like blondes. About this tall with big blue eyes! Mmmmmm! Wonder if Mitzi will be here?"

Mitzi Savrill was there, all right. Soapy spotted her as soon as his eyes adjusted to the dim light.

"Oh, no," Soapy groaned. "Not with *him!*" He pointed toward the center of the floor. "Look, Chip! Look who's with her—Finley! From under my nose! From under both our noses, right?"

Chip nodded absentmindedly. He was thinking it didn't matter very much that Mitzi was with Finley. She had to go with somebody, he guessed. He watched the couples, and the enjoyment in the expressions surprised him. There might be something to this dancing business after all.

CHAPTER 9

A Team Inspired

B. G. ANDERSON loved his only son dearly, but he was perplexed and a little hurt by Eddie's attitude. Their treasured football discussions at dinner were a thing of the past. Eddie hurried through his meals and excused himself with a subdued "Excuse me, please." When B. G. attempted to talk football, his son would murmur something about a lot of studying and head off to his room.

B. G. didn't know what to do. However, a letter from Hunk Thomas, one of the important Booster members, decided his course of action. He would sit through a couple of the freshman practice sessions, anonymously if possible. Maybe he could kill two birds with one stone: check up on the information in Thomas's letter and see why Eddie talked so much about this Hilton kid.

Anderson chose a good day to start. Nelson and Sullivan were looking ahead to the season's opener against Carleton on Saturday morning and were giving the squad a final scrimmage. The freshman starters lined up with Leopoulos at center, Gilmore and Akins at guards, Dean and Maxim at tackles, and Reynolds and Pine at the ends. Finley was at quarterback, McGuire and Rentler were at the half positions, and Roberts was at fullback.

The reserves on offense had English at center, Montague and Waldorf at guards, Cohen and Powell at tackles, Smith and Schwartz at ends, and Hilton, Morris, Carson, and Anderson in the backfield.

The teams were already lined up for the kickoff when Biz Anderson slipped into the bleachers. He easily located Eddie. He'd know his own son a mile away, he guessed. Eddie was huddled with his teammates in a tightly knit circle surrounding Chip a few yards behind the teed-up ball. Biz would have been surprised at the vows, both silent and voiced, that were being made in that huddle.

Every player in the group knew this was his final chance before the start of the season, and each was determined to show he was starting material. Beyond that, however, was a bond of loyalty to one another, a bond that had developed through a realization that the so-called competition for first-string spots was a mockery. They all had vivid memories of the taunts and digs the Booster-protected stars had thrown their way.

"All right, guys," Chip said tersely. "This is it! Give it to them good!"

"Where you gonna kick it, Chip?"

"Right over the fence!"

A responsive yell erupted, echoing their feelings, and they broke from the huddle with grim determination.

Chip caught the ball just right, lifting it high, end over end, and far behind the goal. This wasn't a freshman second-string kickoff, it was college varsity football.

A TEAM INSPIRED

The players on the sidelines appreciated the power behind that kick. So did Eddie's dad.

The stars took over on the twenty and didn't gain an inch. Chip aligned the defense in a seven-man rush. He ignored the potential aerial danger, knowing that was Fireball's greatest weakness. The choice paid off. Red and Soapy smashed in on an angle, taking off from their end positions like sprinters in a hundred-yard dash. Cohen and Powell floated a bit, and Carson and Anderson backed up the holes. On third down and eight, Eddie Anderson met Roberts head-on at the line of scrimmage and flattened him. On the sideline, his dad choked off a cheer just in time and sank back in confusion.

Fireball's punt was directed toward Morris, who had dropped back with Chip. The kick was powerful; the ball carried nearly fifty yards on a line, low and hard. Speed took it on the run, cutting diagonally to his right and in advance of Chip. It wasn't a play, but these two backfield mates knew the maneuver by heart. So did Biggie and Schwartz. They pivoted, after their initial charge, and headed for the left sideline. Speed lateraled to Chip on the dead run, and Chip took off for Biggie and Red.

Running like a scared rabbit, he flashed past midfield and up to the thirty before Finley and McGuire pulled him down. The reserves had really blocked on that play. Anderson had thrown a block on Reynolds that nearly tore the trash-talking end in two.

They raced out of the huddle, and Chip passed on the first play, faking beautifully to Anderson and Carson before hitting Morris in the right flat. It was good for a first down. Again they hustled out of the huddle, and Anderson, playing fullback, crossed behind Morris on the handoff for four yards. Drew Carson made two on a straight lunge over his own tackle, and Chip called for another pass. The Booster stars covered Morris in the right flat when Chip faded to that side but were caught flat-footed when he hit Soapy for a touchdown in the left corner of the end zone.

Soapy had cut straight away from his right-end position, then turned left along the end-zone line, following it to the corner where Chip already had the ball aimed. Chip and Soapy had practiced that one a hundred times.

"Which one of these teams is the Wonder Team?" someone asked sarcastically.

"Who's that tall quarterback? Where they been hiding him?"

"That's Finley! Fireball Finley!"

"Uh-uh. Finley's on the so-called Wonder Team."

At that moment Chip booted the extra point, providing the bleacher coaches with more ammunition.

"He's automatic!"

The Booster stars were burning now. Stinging from the ease with which the reserves had scored, they wanted Finley to receive.

"Now we'll give it to them, Fireball! Show them what a football player really looks like!"

"We'll take care of Hilton this time. He's all they've got!"

Finley shook his head angrily. "I told you guys," he raged. "It's about time you began to put out! They'll make fools out of us if we don't give them a fight!"

"We'll fight! Give us that ball!"

"He'll just kick it over our heads again!"

"Then let's kick to them; it's our choice. Kick it to Hilton!"

An average team lets down following a quick touchdown. But the reserve team wasn't average. It was decidedly below average in sheer ability at several positions. But, with the desire to play and to even scores with a despised opponent, the reserve team was a team inspired. They listened to the bickering of the stars in cold silence, determined to give the Boosters more of the same and chafing at the delay.

"We'll kick!" Finley called to the referee.

On the sideline, in front of the bench, Nelson moved closer to Sullivan. "How about this!" he whispered with delight.

"I know!" Sullivan replied exultantly. "Oh, how I hope, how I hope—"

Nelson nodded. "That would be asking *too* much," he breathed.

"We can *sure* hope," Sullivan muttered.

Finley aimed the ball for Chip, and that's where it went, end over end, down to the fifteen-yard line. The reserves retreated with the kick, formed a perfect wedge, and lit out for all they were worth. They weren't asking for any breaks, and they sure weren't going to give any.

Chip got a good start and headed for the wedge pocket, looking for an opening. Then, just ahead, he saw daylight, an open spot except for Finley, who had followed the kick downfield a little too slowly. That was enough for Chip! He opened the throttle wide and drove straightaway with all the speed and drive at his command. The crash of the blocking was terrific. It was really for keeps. Chip's heart surged with gratitude for the loyalty of his teammates. He'd run this one back if he never carried another ball as long as he lived.

Luck, maybe retributive justice, was with Chip. The hole opened right at the tip of the funnel just as if the coaches had diagrammed each player's movements. Chip sliced through the opening and straight for Finley. Fireball accelerated, too, concentrating on his pumping knees. At the last instant Chip slowed his speed just enough to force his charging opponent to shorten his stride, committing first. He had used this move a hundred times, and as Finley dove for Chip's right leg, Chip cut it to the left. Fireball tried to change direction in the air and clutched desperately at the elusive leg, but he couldn't hold on, and Chip was free.

Chip crossed the goal line, slowed down, and looked for the official. Just as he was turning to hand the ball to the official, Pines, Akins, and Maxim hit him high, low, and in the middle, cutting him down as with a giant scythe. Chip crashed to the ground under the unexpected weight of the flying bodies, and he didn't get up!

There was a brief, dead silence, the exulting cheers of the reserves dying on their lips as the full impact of the dirty play penetrated their senses. They dashed forward, cursing under their breath; then the long-brewing storm exploded.

Chip wasn't out, but he was surprised and dazed. He tried to shield his eyes from the sun and attempted to rise. Pete Pines took care of that, deliberately giving him a sharp elbow to the helmet. A thousand stars flashed about Chip's eyes, but he managed to scramble to his feet. Then, Biggie and Soapy and Eddie Anderson hit Pines and Akins and Maxim all at once, and Chip was knocked back on his face, flattened again in the end zone!

"What is this?" Chip muttered, fighting back to his knees. Through a long, dark tunnel he saw a padded goal post, and he made for that while bodies thrashed above and around him. Somehow, Chip managed to crawl out of that wild melee and, grasping the post, pulled himself upright. As he held tight to the post, his strength returned, surprisingly, suddenly, like that of the boxer who has been near a knockout, but who is saved by the bell and revived by the between-round respite.

A TEAM INSPIRED

Nik Nelson and Jim Sullivan rushed to the squirming pile and began pulling the angry reserves away in every direction from the manhandled Booster stars, with the exception of Biggie Cohen. Biggie was too angry and too much to pull in any direction he didn't want to go.

Fireball Finley, interested only in pulling the combatants apart, dashed up at that instant and pleaded for everyone to stop. Unfortunately, fate directed Fireball right toward Cohen. Biggie didn't overlook the opportunity, landing a straight right to Finley's nose. The powerful blow lifted Fireball from the ground, sent him clawing through the air, and deposited him unceremoniously on his back.

"Break it up!" Nelson shouted. "Stop it, I said! Everybody off this field! Get 'em out of here, Sullivan! Pines! You, Akins, and Maxim report to my office! Now!"

Sullivan led the quieted, thoughtful procession slowly to the locker room. An ominous silence gripped both groups. The usual bantering between friends, the gibes and the jeers that usually flew back and forth across the room, were missing. Chip's leg had begun to stiffen, and his back was sore, but he said nothing, dressing in silence.

Upstairs, Akins, Pines, and Maxim eyed Nelson with apprehensive eyes. The coach was angry.

"This has gone too far! I played football for eight straight years in school and four years in college, and I have never seen a trick as dirty as the one you pulled out there on that field! It's a good thing Hilton wasn't hurt! You know the rules as well as I do, and I'm not buying any cheap excuses like you didn't hear the whistle or you didn't know Hilton had crossed the goal line."

Nelson pointed a trembling finger at them and continued angrily. "You're *supposed* to be football players, not gang members! Now, you get this and get it straight! The next time you step out of line, it's going to be your last or my last, one or the other. Got it? Now get out of here before I throw you out!"

Biz Anderson, standing outside the coaches office, had overheard everything Nelson said. Now he stepped into the room. "Coach, just a minute!" He motioned the players back into the office and then turned to the angry coach.

"You're letting them off too easily, Nelson. They're going to apologize to Hilton or they're packing up! I saw the whole thing! It was despicable! Why, that boy could have been injured for life. Now I'll give you three just two minutes to make up your minds."

There was a deep silence in the room as the three Booster stars considered the significance of Anderson's ultimatum. Each boy knew this man was the most powerful figure in State's Booster Association. His word was law. Deep inside, too, each felt ashamed for his actions on the field.

Football breeds an inner strength, an appreciation of fair play and sportsmanship that may often be hidden by a veneer of bravado or bluffing assurance. But whenever a showdown such as this one brings feelings and emotions to a head, the real spirit and teachings of football come to the surface.

"You're right, Mr. Anderson," Maxim said thickly, his broad face flushed with embarrassment. "I don't know what I was thinking about. I knew he'd crossed the line but something just carried me on—I'm sorry. I'll apologize."

Maxim's two companions agreed, nodding assent with downcast eyes.

"I'll call Hilton," Nelson said, starting for the door.

"No," Anderson demurred. "Suppose we let the players take care of the matter themselves. All right, you three, we'll leave the apologizing up to you."

Nik Nelson was surprised. Perhaps shocked was a better word. He had never expected B. G. Anderson to react this way. The clop-clop of the cleats had scarcely died away before Nik turned to Anderson. Then, in answer to Nelson's questioning glance, he continued.

"Eddie's been raving about Hilton incessantly. In fact, we've almost quarreled about him several times. I thought you'd been tricked by a practice player when you went so far overboard on Hilton at camp, and I attributed Eddie's opinion to inexperience."

He laughed shortly. "I was wrong! That exhibition Hilton put on today sold me. He's everything you said he was, maybe more!"

Nelson, wholly unprepared for Anderson's unexpected turnabout, nodded mechanically as the Booster leader continued.

"It looks as though we'll have to do something about that young man. One thing's certain, he's a real football player!"

Nelson spoke then, relief expressed in the tone of his voice. "I'm sure glad to hear you say that! I've read old sports fiction books about naturals like Hilton—you know, in those classic Frank Merriwell stories—but this kid's the real thing. He can do anything with a football, and he's got all the guts in the world.

"Curly Ralston's always talking about spirit. This kid's the walking definition of that quality. Ever see a bunch of outclassed kids fight like that bunch did this afternoon? They did it for Hilton! He's a natural leader!"

"There are all kinds of leaders, you know, Nik. This boy has been in the center of a lot of this trouble. Maybe he's the wrong kind."

"I don't think so, but . . . well, the reserves sure stick up for him. Ask Eddie."

"I don't have to ask Eddie," Anderson said dryly. "He tells me, constantly!"

There was an uncomfortable silence. Anderson was thinking about the breach Hilton had created between Eddie and himself. He walked to the door and surprised Nelson once again.

"I want you to move Hilton into the Booster house," he said briefly. "The sooner the better! Eddie was right about the Hilton boy."

CHAPTER 10

That's the Way I Want It!

FIREBALL FINLEY loved football. He loved the hard-hitting contact, the competition, and the opportunity to express his flaming spirit in colorful action. Fan adulation and his teammates' recognition of his leadership were important but secondary. A poor last were the extrinsic rewards his prowess assured: the scholarship, books, room, meals, and other fruits that fell his way.

Any renowned athlete would testify enthusiastically that the opportunity for team play and the practice of fair play and sportsmanship are important, but, if pressed, Fireball would have unblushingly added that he had never given that phase of football much thought. And he hadn't until that afternoon, until he'd seen his Booster teammates so callously cut down Chip Hilton. But he was loyal to his supporters, and as he dressed, he tried to find some excuse for their action.

Later, walking home with Akins, Maxim, Reynolds, and the other Booster stars, Fireball heard the rest of the story. The three players somewhat exaggerated their version of Anderson's ultimatum. The stars erupted in angry protest.

"Nothing doing!" Leopoulos declared loudly. "No apology! You understand, Joe?"

Maxim nodded. "Yes, but—"

"No buts!" Roberts interrupted. "We said no apology! And if we stick together, they'll back down. Right, guys?"

The answering chorus expressed the group's approval. Finley kept quiet, trying to interpret his feelings. He couldn't figure out why he felt so uneasy.

Back in the freshman coaches' office, Nik Nelson was trying to analyze his feelings too. He settled comfortably in a chair, and Sullivan found him there a few minutes later.

"Everything all right?" Nelson asked.

"No trouble," Sullivan replied. "Same as usual. Hilton and the others left together, and the stars left just as soon as Pines and the other two got dressed. You know something? This thing's going to really boil over one of these days. We're going to have a real team problem."

"Not if Anderson's newest brainstorm works out."

"Anderson?"

Nelson nodded. "Yes, he followed me up here and ordered Akins, Pines, and Maxim to apologize to Hilton or get out of football."

"I don't understand. How's that going to help?"

"I didn't mean the apology. Anderson wants us to move Hilton into the Booster house."

"What brought that on? He finally agreed with us about Hilton?"

"Yes, he broke down and admitted that Hilton is a real ballplayer."

"What about Cohen?"

"Just Hilton."

Sullivan shook his head. "It won't work," he said skeptically. "Hilton wouldn't blend in with that crowd. He won't go for it. Wait and see!"

Sullivan was right. Chip wasn't interested. Nelson sent for him just before practice the following afternoon and tried to convince him that B. G. Anderson was right, that he should leave Jefferson Hall and move into Anderson House.

"I couldn't do that, Mr. Nelson," Chip protested. "I just couldn't!"

"You mean on account of Cohen and some of the others?"

"Yes, sir, partly. Besides, I have a good job, and I'm getting along fine the way I am. I don't really need any help. In fact, I prefer to work my way through."

Nelson left it that way and told Chip to forget the whole thing. But Nik couldn't get the injustice out of his mind, and he expressed it later to Sullivan.

"It's all wrong, Jim. The whole thing's wrong. Just because a crowd of grandstand quarterbacks, with more money than they know what to do with, want to be sports lords, we have to keep quiet and see kids like Hilton and Cohen treated as though they had some contagious disease. Football's supposed to be a meritocracy. The best players play."

"There isn't anything about merit in this setup," Sullivan muttered grimly. "Man, it did my heart good to see Hilton and his team run all over those arrogant guys yesterday! I'll never forget that as long as I live. Can you believe that kickoff return and those blocks! We couldn't have diagrammed it any better than that! I hope the managers got it on video."

"That reminds me," Nelson said thoughtfully. "I forgot to ask Hilton if those three apologized."

"Probably haven't had time yet. Guess they'll put it off as long as possible."

"They're spoiled," Nelson said dourly. "Spoiled rotten. They could be quite a team, but the Boosters have gone too far."

"I think we ought to pour it on them every chance we get," Sullivan said grimly.

"We can't do much more than we're doing. You know what will happen. They'll sulk and tell lies all over the place, and we'll have every one of their Boosters on our backs."

"So what! I'm getting fed up with outside pressure!"

"Who isn't!" Nelson exclaimed bitterly. "C'mon. Let's have a look at them."

It was more than a look. Sullivan went to town with his agonizing grass drill. Then the players were divided for group work. A solid hour of blocking, tackling, and pulling-out followed. After that, they hit the tackling bags and the charging sled and ended with an extensive signal drill. There wasn't much kidding around. Most of the stars were sullen and rebellious, but they put out enough to avoid an open break. In direct contrast, the reserves were enthusiastic, attacking each task with high, aggressive spirits.

Right after practice, Nelson called B. G. Anderson and relayed the talk he'd had with Chip about moving into Anderson House. Their conversation was evidently unpleasant because Nelson's face was grave and flushed with anger when he hung up.

Sullivan looked up from his desk. "Not good?"

"How about that?" Nelson exploded. "He said I didn't handle it right. Now he wants me to come to his office tomorrow morning."

"Are you going?"

THAT'S THE WAY I WANT IT!

"What else can I do?"

"Wish I knew. C'mon. Let's go home."

Chip and Soapy were sitting on the big porch at Jeff for a few minutes' rest before leaving for work when an upperclassman came striding up the walk.

The slender newcomer spoke with crisp, businesslike tones: "Hi, men. I'm Brett Lindsay and I'm the student council representative in charge of this dorm. Could you arrange to gather all the guys in the house in the main lounge right away?"

Five minutes later they were all assembled, and Lindsay got right down to business, wasting no time. "I have two responsibilities to talk about," he said succinctly. "The first is to acquaint all the residents of Jefferson Hall with the election procedures and to see that officers are elected on the twenty-first. Until that date, I'm in charge as far as student government goes. These handouts outline the election procedure. They should be posted on all the bulletin boards.

"The second responsibility is to get your dorm football team organized and prepared to play out the schedule. I need one of you to take charge of the team until the officers are elected. Any volunteers?"

There was a long silence. Finally Joel Ohlsen rose reluctantly and cleared his throat. "If no one else wants to do it, I could help out until the elections, but that's all. I've got to do some major studying this semester."

"Good," Lindsay said tersely. "Now, these are your duties. First, you present a list of your players to the equipment person in the intramural office, and she'll give you the necessary number of uniforms and gear. Oh, yes, and Jeff is assigned to Station 13 in Alumni Field for practices. There's been some complaints about this dorm's residents roaming around. Please confine your workouts to your own section. That's all! Thanks for your cooperation. So long."

Ohlsen grunted, "That guy must be an economics major."

"Sure is cheap with his words," Schwartz grinned.

"Anyhow, we've got a coach," Caleb Shepherd said. "Now we can do some real practicing."

"We need players more than anything else," Moses Jackson complained. "How come all you freshman team guys had to get assigned to Jeff? How come you don't live in the fancy digs with the rest of the team?"

That got Soapy to thinking, and he and Chip discussed that phase of State football on their way to work.

"Moses is right," Soapy said. "We are the only freshman players living in the regular dorms."

"Not quite," Chip corrected. "Carlson and Hannon live in Garfield, Thomson and Stewart and Garcia, all three, live in Carnegie. Then there's Anderson and O'Neill and Patterson who live at home."

"Anyway, the way things stack up now," Soapy persisted, "the stars all live at the Booster house and they're the regulars."

"Enough for two platoons," Chip said reflectively. It was becoming increasingly apparent that the players known as the stars were most prominent in the teamwork and preparation for the game with Carleton. That night after work, tired as he was, Chip took time to E-mail his mom and tell her that he would see her for sure when the team played Midwestern. He added that he intended to ask Coach Nelson to let him stay home until Sunday. Soapy, Speed, Red, and Biggie were making similar plans. Speed had arranged for Petey Jackson to drive them all back to school Sunday afternoon.

THAT'S THE WAY I WANT IT!

Early the following morning, Nelson started for B. G. Anderson's office. Nik had never been in Anderson's office building in University, but he found just about what he expected: an impressive series of offices taking up several floors with Anderson's private office on the top floor. But Nelson wasn't impressed. He didn't like Biz Anderson and that was that! Period!

Anderson was deeply engrossed in some papers on his desk. He didn't even glance up when Nelson entered the office. Nik stood there uncertainly for a second and then walked to the nearest chair and sat down, nettled by the lack of courtesy. And he was as tight as a drum when Anderson finally looked up, seemingly surprised to find Nelson there.

"Oh, Nelson! Forgive me. Sorry to keep you waiting. I'm up to my ears this morning. Now, what happened?"

"Nothing much. Hilton just said he preferred to remain at Jeff."

"I understand he has to work."

"I don't know about that, but he works down at Grayson's, and he said he liked his job and was getting along fine. Said he didn't need any help."

"How can a student find enough time to work and study and play football?"

"I don't know, but a lot of them do it."

"Boys who have to work their way through school should drop out of football."

Nelson made no reply, waiting for Anderson to continue. Nik was determined to force Anderson himself to make all the decisions about Hilton and any of the other reserves.

"I thought you said most of these outsiders and walk-ons would drop out."

"A few did, Mr. Anderson. But not the serious ones.

Most kids play football because they love the game, not because they get a reward of some kind."

"That may be very well and good when a boy doesn't have to work, but I can't see it when there's an education to be considered. No one can do all those things well. If Hilton chooses to work instead of moving into the house, we'll just have to force him out of football for his own good."

"You mean cut him from the squad?"

"I think he'll cut himself from the squad when he finds out he's going to sit the bench all the time."

"Then you don't want me to use him at all?"

"That's right!"

"How about Cohen and Morris and some of the other kids who live in the dorms?"

"Give them the same treatment. However, and I'm not saying this because of Eddie, I think you'd better give the local boys who live at home a chance to get in at the end of the games if the score's not too close. As far as the rest of them are concerned, the sooner they drop out, the better. They can come out for the varsity next year, and if they're good enough, they'll have their chance then."

"That's pretty rough, Mr. Anderson. Put yourself in their place. Especially Hilton and Morris. They know they're good enough to start, and so does every other player out there. You said yourself Hilton's a great football player. And, in my book, Biggie Cohen is the best tackle on the campus right now, including the varsity. It's pretty hard to justify that action."

"Never mind justifying anything. Let them ride the bench! They'll get tired of that! I've got to keep the Boosters satisfied right now. I got a letter from Hunk Thomas this morning. He thinks Pines is a sure all-American next year on the varsity. The rest of the

THAT'S THE WAY I WANT IT!

Boosters feel the same way about their players. I guess that's the reason everyone's calling this bunch the Wonder Team.

"Now, back to these others. They can dress for the home games, but they're not to make the road trips."

Nelson's jaw muscles tightened, and his lips narrowed into a thin line. But his voice was even and controlled when he spoke. "If that's the way you want it, Mr. Anderson, that's the way it will be."

"That's the way I want it!"

CHAPTER 11

A Misguided Light

NIK NELSON was rooting for Carleton Community College! "Come on," Nik muttered to himself. "Come on, you guys! Score!"

Behind the bench, in the Alumni Field stands, several hundred freshman fans were chanting: "Hold that line! Hold that line! Hold that line!" Behind the end zone and behind the backs of the freshman Wonder Team, the scoreboard read State 12, Visitors 0.

Nik Nelson wanted to win this first freshman game, all right. But he wanted the victory to be so close that he would have some sort of justification for using the Booster stars for the entire game. Nik was especially disturbed about Chip Hilton and Biggie Cohen.

In the first quarter, State scored the first time they got the ball. Too easily. Taking the kickoff, they marched straight down the field on power plays, with Finley skirting right end for the initial touchdown. Fireball missed the point after attempt, but it wasn't considered important because of the ease with which the touchdown had been scored. And when the freshmen scored again in the second quarter to make it 12-0, Nelson began silently hoping for the visitors to give them a game. Now, near the end of the third quarter, it seemed that his prayers were about to be answered.

By accident, the Carleton quarterback stumbled upon the Wonder Team's weakness. He discovered that the star backfield of McGuire, Rentler, Roberts, and Finley were pitiful defenders against a passing attack. Not that Carleton had an outstanding passer or particularly good receivers, but they were good enough. Striking swiftly and unexpectedly through the air, Carleton had backed the vaunted State Wonder Team up against its own goal.

"Hold that line! Hold that line! Hold that line!"

The Carleton quarterback knew what ought to be done, and he did it. He pitched one to the right for three yards, sent his right halfback slashing off left tackle for two, and then hit his left end for six with a quick buttonhook. That put the ball on the freshman three-yard line, first and goal. Finley called time!

The reserves on the bench reacted like puppets to the pull of their strings whenever Nelson looked in their direction. But time and again he looked right past their eager eyes until he caught Sullivan's attention. Coach Sullivan's reassuring nod helped, but not enough. Nik was heartsick. Most coaches would have substituted long before, would certainly have made some change at this psychological moment. But Nelson sat tight, thin-lipped with determination, hoping his team would win but that the game would be close right up to the end. He got his wish! Carleton scored and kicked the extra point just as the third quarter ended and the scoreboard showed State 12, Visitors 7.

Finley elected to receive, hoping to get the offense rolling again. But it was no go. The attack stalled and was held to no gain by a fighting underdog team that had been energized because of the late score and the successful extra point. A touchdown now would mean victory for Carleton! And the Carleton players nearly got it as they struck through the air, time and again, marching right down to the State goal. But they failed to score the winning touchdown only because time ran out.

Chip and the rest of the despondent reserves tramped back to the locker room; this was the first time they'd gotten on the field since the warm-ups. The victorious stars were cocky once again, now that the game was over and in the bag. At that, they weren't too jubilant. There simply wasn't much to gloat about. The game had been saved by the clock, and they knew it.

Most of the spectators who had come to see the Wonder Team overwhelm an inexperienced Carleton squad were disappointed. But they attributed the poor showing to trying too hard. Only a few noted the absence of a good defense for an aerial attack and recognized the kicking weakness. Henry Rockwell and D. H. "Dad" Young, State's athletic director, were in this group. All through the game, Rockwell had expected to see Chip put in so his passing and kicking might turn the dangerous tide. He was frankly amazed.

"I can't understand why they didn't use Chip to throw the ball, to open up their defense," he said thoughtfully. "He's a great passer and he never misses an extra point. I just don't understand it!"

"I do," Young said quietly.

"You do?"

"Yes, I do. All too well! Come along. Maybe I can clear up a few things for you."

They walked silently along with the crowd to Dad's car, saying nothing but listening to the fan talk with deep interest.

"Doesn't look like a Wonder Team to me."

"Sure don't have a defense against the pass."

"No pass attack either."

"I thought Finley was supposed to be a kicker!"

"What was wrong with his kicking?"

"What was good? Missed both tries after those easy TDs."

"He averaged almost fifty yards on his punts!"

"Sure! And the other team ran them back twenty or thirty yards each time too."

"Yeah, he kicks too low, so his coverage can't get down the field before the other team sets up."

Rockwell and Young exchanged knowing smiles but said nothing until they were in the athletic director's car. "Rock, I guess you've been wondering what happened up here since last May when I spoke at your sports banquet in Valley Falls."

Rockwell nodded. "Yes, Dad," he said, "I have."

"Well," Young continued, "I turned in my resignation as director of athletics because of the Booster Association. But Prexy persuaded me to take it back. He doesn't like the current setup himself, but he thinks it should be given a chance before he puts his foot down."

"I don't follow."

"Well, alumni and boosters trying to run athletic programs is nothing new. It's always a tough balancing act. The great majority of our State University alumni and boosters are great folks and real assets to the school and our athletes. But this summer, a few of them did some behind-the-scenes maneuvering and got their tentacles in the freshman pilot program.

"I was away on vacation and didn't know anything about it until I got back. Dean Murray called me into his office then and told me that all the athletic details for the pilot program—except for the satisfaction of university entrance requirements, following the athletic association by-laws, and the maintenance of the required scholastic standing—had been turned over to the Booster Association for administration."

"Just what does that mean?"

"It means that all athletic income and all expenses from the entire pilot program, scholarships, supervision of the athletes, and the hiring and firing of the freshman athletic staff are in their hands."

"I see," Rockwell said gravely. "In effect, the entire freshman pilot program is set apart from the rest of the school."

"Exactly. By the way, have you met a man by the name of Anderson?"

"I don't think so."

"You will! And be careful when you do. B. G., or 'Biz' as they call him, is their guiding light or rather their misguided light. He's got more money than he knows what to do with, and he's organized a special group to develop relationships with freshman players. Each one donated scholarship funds to the university earmarked for incoming freshman athletes in football, basketball, and baseball.

"The Booster Association even created the selection committee to determine which incoming freshman athletes would receive the Booster scholarships. So each Booster feels he is directly responsible for one of the players. Just from the short time I've observed the freshman football team, it's obvious that each of these Boosters thinks his athlete is tops. And if the athlete doesn't play, the coaches will surely hear about it."

"You mean Nelson and Sullivan?"

"That's right! They were hired by the association! Who knows what the basketball season is going to be like."

The car grew silent as Rockwell thought over all he'd been told. His tightly compressed lips and the deep frown lines between his snapping black eyes affirmed his concentration. If Dad Young knew Rock better, he would have recognized the danger signs.

"So that's it," Rockwell said harshly. "If an athlete doesn't have an influential Booster backing him, he doesn't play."

"That's right!"

Rockwell squirmed restlessly. "I never expected to find a situation like this at State University. I'll bet the voters of this state would be up in arms if they knew about this nonsense."

"Maybe yes and maybe no," Young said cynically. "It's been my experience that the voters applaud rather than condemn the saving of our taxpayer's use of public funds. No, Rock, if you analyze the idea, it's pretty hard to find the flaws. Private donations to the university guarantee tuition, room, meals, and fees for a deserving individual."

"The absence of university control is certainly a big enough flaw. These athletes represent the school, and the school should be in charge," Rock said.

"Look, Rock. I feel the same way. But when you try to tell an outsider it's wrong for an individual or a group to pay coaches' salaries and cover the educational expenses for a bunch of young kids, why, they laugh at you."

"Does all this mean that I'm employed by the association?"

Young grinned. "No, Rock. You're a full-fledged member of the faculty."

FRESHMAN QUARTERBACK

"Does Curly Ralston understand the setup?"

"He clearly supports the goals of the freshman pilot program. But he hasn't been here long enough to know how involved the Boosters are in the freshman program. Frankly, I think he's an extremely decent man, and I've been on the point of discussing the matter with him several times."

Rockwell nodded. "I think you're right. You know," he said thoughtfully, "Ralston strikes me as the kind of coach who wants the best eleven players out on the field playing the game. I don't think he'd stand for favoritism."

"I agree. Suppose we have dinner with him some evening and sound him out. I'll bet he doesn't know anything about this freshman team situation."

"Probably not, Dad," Rockwell said wryly, hopping out of the car, "but I wouldn't want to bother him with this right now. He's got his own troubles. Facing a major schedule with no kicker and no real passer is a tough assignment to have your first year on the job. Guess I'd better hustle over and see if I can help out. I'll see you at the game."

Two games of football in one day would be too much for some people, but they weren't for Dad Young. He was in the stands again that afternoon; so were Chip and his friends. And they had something to cheer about because the varsity won its first game of the season, beating the Golden Flashes by a score of 13-10. Soapy, Red, and Speed joined in the student celebration that followed, but Chip and Biggie ate early and went back to the dorm to do some studying. Later that night, Chip remained in his room, ignoring the many persistent pleas for him go to the movies, to the dance, to the mall, to the Student Union, or "just out." The best response anyone got from him was, "Maybe I'll drop in later."

A MISGUIDED LIGHT

After they left, Chip E-mailed his mom. He told her about the game and explained that few of the reserves got to play because the game was too close for much substituting. Then he told her not to expect to see him play much in the game against Midwestern. When he finished, all desire to study had vanished, and he decided to join some of the guys at the union. Outside in the hall, he heard the rumble of a voice. He listened until he recognized Joel Ohlsen's voice and then tapped on the door.

"Come in," Ohlsen called.

Chip found Joel all alone, striding back and forth reading aloud from a paper. "What's up?" Chip asked. "What are you reading?"

"My speech! My campaign speech!"

"Campaign speech?"

"Yep. That student council guy said he was putting my name up for class president and told me to prepare a speech. This is it! What could I do?"

Chip listened to Joel repeat his speech five straight times and then suggested they take a break and see what was going on at the union. When they returned, Chip had to listen to it again. Just before midnight, they both agreed it was in pretty good shape. Then Biggie, Red, and Speed returned, and Joel had to go through it again for their benefit. Soapy, barely under the wire for the midnight curfew, insisted upon passing judgment too. By this time, Chip knew the speech as well as Joel did.

Back in their room, Soapy kept Chip awake for what seemed like hours, talking about the dance and Mitzi. He had finally gotten to dance with the girl of his dreams.

"And, you know, Chip, she's pretty good! Not bad at all! *At all!*" Soapy was still rambling on about Mitzi when Chip finally fell asleep.

Monday morning brought tragedy to Jefferson Hall. Chip was awakened by Speed Morris at seven o'clock. "Chip! Wake up! Joel's sick! He can't talk! He wants to see you."

"Sick?"

"Yeah, sore throat! Can't speak above a whisper. He's in knots about the election."

"I'll bet he is," Chip observed, scrambling into his clothes. "Wake Soapy, and we'll take Joel to the student health center."

"We just got back from there. The doctor said it'll be three or four days before his voice is normal. Joel wants to see you."

Speed was right. Joel couldn't talk above a whisper and even that required an effort. Speed got a pencil and Joel scribbled a short note and handed it to Chip. Chip read the words slowly, shaking his head as the meaning of the message became clear.

"Nothing doing! Not me!" he objected, looking at Joel.

Soapy grabbed Joel's note and read the words aloud.

"Chip, you know the speech better than I do. Please make it for the sake of Jeff. You'll be elected for certain. I know the guys will get behind you. You'd make a better class president than I would anyway."

Soapy nodded his head enthusiastically. "He's right, Chip! You'll win! Joel's right! It's a no-brainer! Right, guys? I'll get everybody. Be right back!"

"Joel's right, Chip. You gotta do it for Jeff."

"Yeah, we want that presidency!"

"What d'ya say, Chipper?"

Chip shook his head stubbornly, and he was still protesting when Soapy returned, followed by a bewildered and sleepy mob. The chattering jester had awakened practically every Jeff resident. This was a crisis, and Soapy had impressed the guys with its seriousness by repeating in room after room, "Wake up! We gotta get Chip Hilton to make the election speech! Joel Ohlsen's sick! Come on, get up! Chip's in Joel's room. Hurry up!"

The second-floor hallway was jammed by this time, and the buzzing Jeffs wouldn't accept Chip's no. In desperation, he finally agreed. As soon as the words were out of his mouth, he regretted the decision. But it was too late. The die was cast.

Chip's acceptance united the Jeff freshmen more quickly than a hundred regular meetings. They made their plans quickly and enthusiastically.

"Just as soon as the class ends, beat it! No talking to the professors after class today. We *gotta* win this!"

The bell set Jeff's electorate in motion in the same way that a sprinter reacts to the crack of a starting pistol. Jeff got the coveted position in the center of the Student Union and went to work. It was all the result of enthusiastic organization.

It was noisy! Each group cheered wildly for its candidate. Ohlsen was fourth on the list. When Joel's name was called, Chip walked to the front on rubbery legs. He explained his presence to the student council chairman, who then announced that, due to illness, a substitute speaker was delivering the address of Jeff's candidate, Freshman Joel Ohlsen.

"My name is Chip Hilton," Chip began. "I live in Jefferson Hall and have known Jeff's candidate for many years. In fact, we grew up together and have been close friends all our lives. Joel Ohlsen will make State's freshman class a terrific president! He is an excellent student, a fine speaker, a good football player, and a great guy to be around. He is coaching Jeff's football team and has served as Jeff's coordinator since our arrival on campus.

"I have tried to master his thoughts and words, but I am sure you will understand that I am only a poor substitute for the originator of the speech."

Chip had forgotten everyone now and was completely absorbed by his resolve to do a good job for Joel. And it was easy because it came from his heart. This was for the Joel Ohlsen Chip liked best to remember, the jovial playmate of elementary school days. As Chip talked, the vibrant tones of his voice expressed all the respect and hopes he held for his hometown friend. His words rang with feeling, hope, and sincerity.

Soapy, Biggie, Red, Speed, and their brother Jeffs thrilled at Chip's impassioned delivery. As their pride grew, the crowd began to respond enthusiastically to this freshman who was pleading so fervently for his friend. They expressed their feelings with cheers when Chip finished, leaping to their feet and applauding him every step of the way back to his seat.

There were other speakers, some girls, some guys, all saying the usual things, but not one came close to matching Chip's eloquent sincerity. As hoped, Joel Ohlsen, in a landslide victory, won the presidency of State's freshman class! But to the surprise of everyone except the freshman voters, a write-in candidate won the office of vice president. His name was Chip Hilton.

CHAPTER 12

Alumni Quarterbacks

BIGGIE COHEN took a long drink from his rich chocolate shake and winked humorously at Chip. Soapy had picked up his biology lab notebook and was walking confidently to the cashier's desk. Holding out the lab book, Soapy flashed his best smile and pleaded for Mitzi's help.

"Mitzi, you know I can't draw those little, tiny lines with my big, thick fingers. It takes a delicate touch. Look at these big hands! Would you mind—"

"Yes, I mind! I'm busy! I've got my own classwork to take care of. Beat it!"

Chip caught Mitzi's mischievous grin and smiled in return. He'd been getting a lot of smiles from the cashier's desk during the past few days. And he owed it all to Soapy. The incorrigible funster kept creating situations that allowed Mitzi to bestow her smiles lavishly in Chip's direction. Chip hadn't found the attention too difficult to take. In fact, as a result, he read the flier in the Student Union announcing various types of dance classes about five times and had even stood outside one of the dance rooms in the fine arts building watching a ballroom dancing class in session.

Going back to Jeff that evening with Biggie and Soapy, the conversation was all about the game at Midwestern the following Saturday. The Valley Falls veterans looked to that game with gloom, even foreboding. All their hometown friends would be there—to see them sit the bench, probably for the whole game. Surprisingly, Soapy was the first to broach the subject closest to their hearts.

"What if we don't play at all?"

Biggie shrugged. "Then we don't play!"

"But what are we gonna say? How we gonna explain it?"

"We don't have to say anything. We're riding the bench. Period!"

"That's all right for the rest of us," Soapy commented bitterly. "But it sure isn't right for you two guys."

"What makes us any different?" Chip asked.

"Ability for one thing!" Soapy retorted. "Sheer ability! Everyone knows that. Even Fireball Finley and his wonder boys know you belong on the first team. Wonder Team? They make me wonder, all right!"

"The only thing we can do," Chip said resignedly, "is give a good account of ourselves tomorrow afternoon in the scrimmage. Maybe Nelson and Sullivan will give us a chance Saturday if we look good tomorrow."

"*We've* looked good before," Biggie replied shortly. "It didn't seem to get us very far."

"Maybe things will be different now," Chip said hopefully. "At least we can try."

They tried. And how they tried! This was the first scrimmage since Chip had been injured, and the play pattern was almost the same. Chip kicked off over the goal line, and the reserves held. Finley kicked on the fourth down, and Chip ran it back to midfield. He passed on the first play to Soapy, who was down to the thirty before he was knocked out of bounds. Speed made five tough yards over left tackle behind the superb blocking of Cohen and Schwartz. Chip tossed a bullet pass to Speed in the flat, and the powerful back carried to the ten. Chip ran a fake pass to the four-yard line and then used a soft lob to Schwartz from his quarterback position after a fake into the line for the score. He kicked the point after, and the reserves led, 7-0.

The stars were really burning now. Finley elected to receive, and Chip again kicked the ball into the end zone. The stars took charge on the twenty, and for the first time Fireball really received good blocking from his lazy teammates. Chip tackled the hard-running quarterback on the forty and brought him down with a crash.

"That's the way to hit, Hilton," Fireball grinned when he scrambled to his feet.

The stars began to hit too. And they began to roll. Finley was now smart enough to keep away from Biggie Cohen's side of the line, but he didn't spare Powell at the other tackle. Chip showed a seven-front defense, playing his linebackers close behind the tackles, and that helped some. But the stars were really blocking now; they moved steadily down the field. The score was inevitable. The reserves fought for every inch, but the superior weight and experience of the hand-picked opponents were too much. They scored on straight, run-right-at-the-opponent, power football. Fireball flubbed the extra point. The score: Stars 6, Reserves 7.

Chip elected to receive and ran the ball back to the forty where he was gang tackled. Underneath the pile of bodies, Chip was pinned helplessly, unable to move. Then he caught it from all sides. Elbows jabbed into his neck, legs, and stomach, but he said nothing. He took it without a word. But he made up his mind that he wasn't going to be caught in a pile again. He'd stick to the open field. Passes, reverses, laterals, and kicking.

It paid off. The reserves moved downfield and were soon knocking at the door again. The stars held on the thirty, and Chip broke their hearts by booting the ball cleanly through the uprights with a three-point field goal. That made it 10-6, and that was the score when Nelson called it a day.

It was a victory for the reserves, all right. They left in a group, at peace with the world and with the stars too.

"If that performance doesn't convince them of our football desire and effort," Soapy said delightedly, "we might as well quit."

"It was a good win," Anderson agreed.

"You guys look good!" Drew Carson chimed in. "Maybe I should move out of Anderson House. Seems to me *you* guys have got the Wonder Team."

Good news was waiting at the dorm too. Adam Russo came rushing in a few minutes after they got home to tell them Jeff had defeated Hanna Hall, 6-0.

"Imagine me calling the winning play," he said grinning. "And with only twenty seconds to play!"

"Yeah," Schwartz needled, "and you're a guard too."

Chip thought Friday would never come. When it did, he wished it hadn't. The trip roster posted on the freshman bulletin board didn't include a single reserve name! That is, with the exception of O'Neill and Patterson. Eddie Anderson's name had been listed there, but someone had crossed it out. Perhaps rubbed out would be more correct. It was barely legible.

ALUMNI QUARTERBACKS

Eddie Anderson could have explained the crossed-out name from the traveling squad list. In fact, a little later, he explained it to his dad at the dinner table.

"All set for tomorrow, Eddie?" B. G. asked pleasantly.

Eddie came right to the point. "If you mean the trip to Midwestern, Dad, I'm not going."

"Not going? What do you mean? You're supposed to go, aren't you?"

"I *was* on the list, if that's what you mean."

"Then why aren't you going?"

"Because I've always believed the best players should play, and since that isn't true as far as freshman football is concerned, I'm not interested."

"Eddie, I don't understand this. I thought you'd be proud to be on the team. To make the trips! To represent your school!"

"I would if the team was selected on the basis of fairness. If the players *earned* their positions. I'm sorry, Dad, it's no honor to be a member of a team where favoritism is the deciding factor in picking the team. No thanks, I'd rather play dorm football, and I would if I lived in one of the halls."

"Does this mean you've quit football?"

"No, sir. I'm going to keep going to all the practices and scrimmages. The way it stands right now, I'm a regular on the best team, even if we don't play in the games. I guess it's no use for me to tell you about it, but we whipped the pants off your Wonder Team again Wednesday afternoon. And you know who did most of the damage? Or nearly all? Chip Hilton! We ran 'em crazy—"

Eddie's father pushed his chair away from the table and stood up. His face was flushed purple with anger, but he held himself in control. "I won't discuss that name again! I gave him every chance to do the right thing, and he proved to be ungrateful and unappreciative. I won't have him discussed in this house. That's final!"

Eddie was on the point of saying something right then that would have brought his relationship with his father to a climax. But he thought better of it, left the house, and headed for Grayson's. The dinner conversation had brought Eddie close to making a decision he had been thinking about for some time. Eddie had just about reached the limit of his endurance.

He walked in on a gloomy bunch at Grayson's. Chip greeted him pleasantly enough, but Eddie could tell that he was hurt. Soapy was downcast but curious about the crossed-off name.

"Hey, Eddie, you see where someone tried to cross your name off the list?"

"Yes, I saw it. I should have. I did it myself."

Soapy's jaw dropped. "*You* did it! *Why?*"

Eddie grinned, nodding toward the cashier's desk. "Because I didn't want to go. You see, Mitzi and I are going dancing tomorrow night."

"Not *even* in your dreams!" Soapy's moan brought a laugh from Chip and a smile from Mitzi. Soapy moaned again but cheered up quickly enough when Eddie reassured him Mitzi was saving two dances for him.

The Booster stars made it a point to drop in that night too. They wanted to talk about the trip, and they wanted an audience. Particularly Chip Hilton and Soapy Smith.

"Wonder if there's a good movie playing in Valley Falls," Bebop Leopoulos said innocently.

"I'd rather go to the dance they've arranged for us," Pete Pines remarked. "Especially with Finley. He draws the girls at a dance."

"Nelson will probably let us stay out until two or three o'clock after the beating we're going to give those Prep wimps," Sean Reynolds said loudly.

"Well, I gotta go back and pack," Lonnie Akins boasted. "Gotta look my best for the first trip of the year. C'mon, guys, we need our beauty rest."

The pointed remarks hit their targets, but Chip and Soapy weren't talking. They kept busy with their customers and bided their time. But they were seething inside. Mitzi Savrill didn't help, although her question was asked in the best of faith.

"Bring us something from Valley Falls, will you, Chip?"

"I'm not going," Chip replied briefly. "I wasn't on the list."

"Oh, I'm sorry," Mitzi said quickly. "I didn't know. Aren't you going anyway?"

"No," Chip answered. "I'm not going anywhere except Jeff."

Soapy looked from Chip to Mitzi and back again. "I'm not going anywhere either," he added sadly.

That night the old Valley Falls crowd gathered in Chip and Soapy's room and sat there a long time without speaking. They were a glum lot, sick at heart, and homesick.

"I called Petey," Speed said forlornly. "Told him the whole story and that we weren't going to make the trip. He promised to tell Doc Jones and John Schroeder."

"Well, at least we can sleep late," Soapy said resignedly.

"Not me," Chip said abruptly. "I'm going out to watch Jeff beat Adams."

Chip had company. The whole crowd was there cheering on the Jeffs. The Jeffs needed it, too, because Adams was stronger and heavier. Joel Ohlsen was still sick in bed so Chip took the coaching reins, and it was a good thing he did. Going into the last minute of play, the game was scoreless with Adams in possession on its own ten-yard line. Jeff took a time-out, and Chip outlined a play for an attempted blocked punt to Caleb Shepherd and Moses Jackson.

"Caleb, you stand about three yards behind the center of the line. When Moses and Adam pull the center and the guard apart, you run right up that alley with your hands up in the air. Run right up the kicker's leg, you hear?

"Now, Moses, you're going to pull the center to the right. And, Adam, you're going to pull their right guard to the left, your left! Got it?

"OK. Now go in there and block that punt and fall on it! Remember, you've got a touchdown if you fall on it!"

Caleb Shepherd proved he could follow instructions. He timed it just right, sprinting through the gaping hole and up the lane just as if he had been playing football for years. He was thrilled when the ball hit him flush on his outstretched hands. The blocked punt bounded back over the goal line. The Adams dorm fullback fell on the ball in the end zone. A safety! The two-point margin was as big as a hundred! It meant victory for Jeff!

Chip got a good riding then. A ride on the shoulders of his brother Jeffs; he felt as good about it as if he had just been elected captain of the freshman team.

Just about that time, the State freshman team bus passed through Valley Falls on its way to Midwestern Prep. When the team hit the field for warm-ups, many Valley Falls football fans were already filling the visitor stands.

They wanted to see this freshman Wonder Team that Hilton, Cohen, and Morris weren't good enough to make. *This* they had to see! This Wonder Team!

ALUMNI QUARTERBACKS

So they sat on their hands and analyzed the team on the field with cool, detached football appreciation. They were well qualified. They knew the caliber of Midwestern, a team that had been depleted by graduation; a team that had been pushed all over the field a week earlier by their own Valley Falls High School kids in a scrimmage. The conclusion was unanimous. This was no Wonder Team! So what was going on at State?

They didn't say much; they just mulled it over in their minds and started home with incredulous glances at the scoreboard. The 24-21 victory State's highly publicized freshmen had achieved, coming from behind in the last quarter, was hardly a recommendation to football immortality. No, there was something out of line here.

Alvin Hoffman, Midwestern's clever young coach, was thinking the same thing. Hoffman was a former State star and knew Nelson and Sullivan well. And he sure knew Chip Hilton. The previous year Chip had starred for Valley Falls High and completely dominated the play on this very field against the best team Prep had fielded in years.

Hoffman congratulated Nelson and Sullivan on the victory and then exploded. "You guys in your right minds?"

"What do you mean?"

"What's this Wonder Team hype!"

"Look, Al," Nelson said with chagrin, "you understand how publicity guys are, building up things for newspaper stories."

"I can understand that," Hoffman said evenly, "but what I can't understand is you two guys letting alumni quarterbacks pick the team. How come Chip Hilton didn't make this team? Break both his legs? Fall off the planet?"

CHAPTER 13

Soapy's Close Encounter

RED SCHWARTZ pounced on the phone at the first ring. At that, he was only a step ahead of Soapy. Holding the receiver with one hand, he fought Soapy off with the other.

"Yes, this is 212 . . . Sure enough! . . . That's right! This is Red . . . Oh, sure . . . Chip . . ." Red pushed Soapy playfully in the face and got back to the receiver. "Yeah, Sweets, for you . . . Sure."

"Who is it?" Soapy demanded feverishly. "Gimme that phone! It's for me!"

Red pushed him away again. "Shhhh, it's for Chip!"

"It's a divine babe!"

"So what! She wants Chip!"

"So, I'm his roommate. Chip trusts me."

"Well, I don't! Hey, Chip! Phone!" Red yelled down the hallway.

Chip managed to squirm between the two straining bodies and get the receiver within six inches of his ear.

SOAPY'S CLOSE ENCOUNTER

Soapy and Red had him penned in and were fighting for the best position.

"Hello! . . . Aw, come on, guys . . . Yes, this is Chip . . . Oh, sure! Mitzi!"

Soapy clasped his hands and expertly thrust Schwartz aside. It was a perfect offensive arm block. Then Soapy banged his head against the receiver straining to hear. "Mitzi!" he breathed.

Chip was shaking his head. "No, sorry, Mitzi," he said lamely, "I don't think I can . . . Well, I—"

Soapy grabbed the phone. "*Yes,* yes, yes, yes! Sure, Mitzi . . . where? . . . Your house? Both of us? . . . Of course, I know where it is! We'll be there! Six o'clock sharp! See ya!"

Soapy dropped the receiver and flopped down on the unmade bed. "Oh, man! She asked me to dinner! Do I rate or what!"

"You rate?" Schwartz ridiculed. "You mean overrate! I thought she asked Chip."

"Well, so what? We're roomies. Where one goes the other goes! Besides, that doesn't mean anything. Classy women are subtle, you know that. They camouflage things. Mitzi's using Chip to get to me. You know what I mean?"

"I know what you'd like to mean."

Soapy had a thick skin. And he needed it. In five minutes everyone on the second floor knew that Chip Hilton and Soapy Smith had been invited to dinner at the Savrills'.

"It's French, you know," Soapy explained. "Like escadrille, quadrille, and that sort of stuff. French aristocracy from Alsace-Lorraine, I'm told, wherever that is! Nobles! Kings! Counts—"

Speed interrupted. "Why would they want to have dinner with a no-account like you? Maybe they want you to serve dinner!"

Soapy brushed off Speed and continued enthusiastically, "Well, these French folks sent an escadrille over here when we were fighting England. And that's how the Savrills got here!"

"An escadrille?"

"You know—a flotilla of ships."

"Thank goodness for the Savrills' escadrille!"

"Soapy, are you falling asleep again in that history class?" Red joked.

Soapy didn't mind, but Chip wasn't going to listen to their routine again and loudly announced, "We're just having dinner with her family."

"Mitzi won't be home?" Speed needled.

Later, Chip had to admit it wasn't so bad after all. The Savrills lived in a beautiful red-brick house set back from the street and surrounded by the well-kept shrubbery and landscaping that graced every house and lawn in University.

Mitzi's parents were friendly and gracious. Chip soon felt at home. Soapy, always at home anywhere, took care of his own orientation. After dinner, they all sat in the comfortable living room, and the boys, in front of the glowing fireplace, discussed their college plans and ambitions. Chip had never spent such a pleasant evening. That is, until he reached Jeff and followed Soapy up to their room.

The room was a sight! Pictures of girls were taped on every inch of space on the walls. Lipstick covered the pillows and towels. Strong, heavy perfume filled the room. Mitzi's name was scrawled everywhere. Soapy didn't seem to mind. He was walking on air, dreaming dreams, floating through the room with the greatest ease.

SOAPY'S CLOSE ENCOUNTER

Oddly enough, Red Schwartz, Biggie Cohen, and Eddie Anderson were the only guys around, and they appeared just as surprised about the room as Chip.

Then the phone rang!

Red won the race easily this time. He seemed almost to be expecting the call. "It's for you, Soapy! A girl with a familiar southern accent!"

"No!" Soapy gulped. "You sure? Am I popular or what?"

He grabbed the receiver and poured as much of himself into the conversation as possible. "Hello! Hello!" he called breathlessly. "This is Soapy Smith! . . . Oh, hi, Mitzi! . . . It was wonderful! . . . You mean it? . . . What time? . . . You're kidding, right? . . . You really mean it? . . . Tonight? . . . I don't know. . . Where?

"Mitzi, couldn't we make it some other night? We have to be in at midnight, and it's after eleven now . . . Of course I do! But isn't it awfully dark around there? . . . Afraid? Me? Never! . . . OK, I'll be there! . . . Yes, I'll remember. I'll light a match by the main gate of the stadium. OK, I'll be there in five minutes, ten max!"

Soapy, muttering a mile a minute, dashed out into the hall, thought of something, dashed back, and rummaged through his desk. Then, in desperation, he asked Chip for a match. "I gotta have a match! I gotta have a fist full of matches!"

"You know I don't smoke," Chip laughed. "What in the world do you need matches for? And where are you going?"

Red seemed to be enjoying Soapy's dilemma. "Wait here," he drawled. "I think I've got some in my room. I'll only be an hour or two."

"I can't wait that long! I can't even wait a millisecond! Oh, for a match! My kingdom for a match!"

"I thought it was a horse."

"Cut the funny stuff, Biggie. This is serious!"

Soapy pushed Red into his room and waited impatiently while Red searched fruitlessly through his desk. "No match!" Red announced carelessly. "How about that!"

"Maybe in Joel's room," Cohen said.

Soapy clutched at his wrist, feverishly gazed at his watch, then rushed into Joel and Speed's room. He was back in a second, waving a matchbook in the air as he dashed for the steps. "Thanks! See you! Gotta run! I'm late!"

Soapy had barely reached the bottom of the steps before Biggie grabbed Chip by the arm and propelled him toward the stairs. "C'mon," he whispered hoarsely. "We gotta hurry!"

Chip didn't know what it was all about, but he followed Biggie, Red, and Eddie, who seemed to know exactly where they were going and why. They weren't a minute too soon as they panted through the main stadium gate and into the darkness.

"Shhhhh," someone hissed. "Here he comes!"

Chip heard Soapy's quick footsteps on the sidewalk and, almost as quickly, made out a shadowy figure that paused uncertainly by the ticket box in the open passageway.

"Mitzi?" Soapy called.

"Shhhhh," the soft voice whispered. "Light the match so I know it's you."

Soapy fumbled excitedly with the matchbook and struck a match. Out of the darkness a vague, shadowy figure in a long coat walked slowly toward Soapy.

"I just had to see you once more," the voice cooed. "Come closer."

Then it happened!

SOAPY'S CLOSE ENCOUNTER

A firecracker exploded so suddenly that Chip nearly jumped out of his skin. Before he fully realized the source of the explosion, he got another shock.

A second figure emerged from the shadows shining a blinding light in Soapy's eyes. Soapy froze, not knowing what to do.

"So you're seeing freshmen, Mitzi?" The deep voice thundered. "He's not even French!"

Then Soapy heard ominous growling coming from behind the shadowy figure with the light. "You know what happens to freshmen around here. They become *fresh* meat! Sic him, Ivan."

"Run, Soapy, run! Save yourself! Don't worry about me!" the long-coated figure drawled.

Soapy's feet scarcely touched the ground! He fled so fast that the streetlights barely caught his flying heels. The shouts and hoots of the pursuing Jeffs seemed to lend impetus to his speed. Soapy left them behind as if they were standing still.

Minutes later the jubilant plotters arrived at Jeff and pounded upstairs just in time to grab by baseball bat out of Soapy's hands.

"How's Mitzi? Is she safe? Did that thing go after her? I've got to help her!" Soapy gasped, his eyes wide with fear.

The hysterical laughter that greeted the question scared Soapy still more. It took half an hour to convince him it had all been a joke—at his expense—once again. He finally calmed down when teammate Alonzo Patterson bounded into the room with Ivan, his friendly Doberman.

"Soapy, you should've seen your face! But your scream scared poor little Ivan. He may never growl again," Speed chuckled. "Alonzo, you were great!"

Red couldn't stand it any longer. "Speed, your sultry southern accent had me convinced. How 'bout you Soapy?"

FRESHMAN QUARTERBACK

Soapy chuckled to himself. It had been a good show and he'd performed his part as expected, but Ivan sure was a surprise! But he promised himself that someday he'd personally teach Speed Morris how to sound like a girl. Then he began to plan a "blind date" for Fireball Finley. And Soapy decided right then and there he'd get a real girl to do the talking on the phone.

Some coaches ease up on their regulars on the Monday following a Saturday victory while others prefer to work them hard to correct errant plays and missed opportunities and to avoid overconfidence. Nelson had intended to pour it on the stars, but he caught their air of superiority and heard a few of their cutting remarks about Valley Falls, so he dismissed them right after Sullivan's grass drill and "three laps!"

The reserves caught it then. Not because Nelson and Sullivan wanted to punish them, but because they wanted to give these players some long-overdue attention. Besides, the two coaches were still smarting from Alvin Hoffman's caustic remarks. They were facing the disturbing fact that they were violating one of football's basic principles: a player stands on his own feet on the gridiron. The best man should get the call. This realization did not help their self-esteem.

Later, as they were dressing, all the thoughts they had stored up since Saturday surfaced. Nelson took the lead. "If you had to pick the best offensive team we could put on the field, Jim, how would it stack up?"

Sullivan grinned wryly. "That's easy," he said lightly. "I'd start with Hilton at quarterback and Cohen at left tackle and then choose nine other guys blindfolded."

"Starting tomorrow," Nelson said decisively, "we're picking the best eleven for the starting team."

"You're making a mistake," Sullivan warned. "You know what will happen. Every one of those prima donnas will run to his Booster, and we'll hear about it."

"We'll have fun and a hot football team while it lasts."

It wasn't so much fun after all. After the grass drill, Nelson launched his bombshell.

"We're going to do a little shaking up of the team. Jim and I are disgusted with some of your attitudes, and we've decided on the following offense for the time being: at the ends, Schwartz and Smith; tackles, Cohen and Maxim; guards, Gilmore and Montague; center, English; Hilton at quarterback; Morris and McGuire at the halves; and Finley at fullback.

"Jim, you set up the rest of the squad members in an offense and defense, and then both groups run signals. Adjust the individual spots as you want. We'll scrimmage Wednesday. All right, now, first team offense, let's go!"

It wasn't an open rebellion, but it was as close as possible without an actual mutiny. Finley muttered something about never playing fullback in his life and Nelson heard him.

"A quarterback should be able to play any position in the backfield, Finley," Nelson said coldly.

"But I'm a quarterback."

"That's your opinion. I happen to think otherwise."

Sullivan had the toughest job, but he seemed to relish the assignment. Akins, Reynolds, and Leopoulos were sullen, and Pete Pines was openly rebellious. Pines didn't move when Sullivan told him to take the right-end position. He just stared contemptuously at him for a second and then turned deliberately away. That was what the burly line coach was waiting for. It gave him the opening he wanted.

"Don't mope around here, Pines. Hit the showers! All right, the rest of you get going!"

But the trouble wasn't over. Akins, Leopoulos, and Reynolds followed Pines and started off the field. "Where you going?" Sullivan demanded. When there was no reply, he took after them, catching up with the sullen quartet before they had gone five yards. "Just for that," he said angrily, "you're all suspended from the team for your insolence. When you want to play football again and follow instructions, report to Coach Nelson in his office. Until then, you're through. Turn in your uniforms!"

That jarred the first-string players and filled them with hustle. Chip felt the tension whenever he handed off to Finley or McGuire, but the team's enthusiasm as a whole and his sheer love of the game were enough to make him forget everything. He was on the first team at last.

Wednesday afternoon the new freshman starters ran roughshod over the reserves. Not only because they were a better team, but because the demoted stars played half-hearted football, putting out just enough to get by. Chip's passing and kicking were a revelation, and Finley suddenly found himself breaking away for two long runs. Fireball almost seemed to like his new assignment. At least, there was nothing in his play to indicate that he was rebellious. In fact, he felt so good after the scrimmage that he decided to drop by Grayson's and visit with his favorite dancing partner.

That night, however, the dam broke. Bebop Leopoulos and Sean Reynolds circulated a petition that everyone in the Booster house had signed. When Fireball arrived, Reynolds thrust the paper into his hands. "Here! Sign this!"

Finley took it in at a glance but continued to scan the paper while he tried to collect his thoughts. He knew he was stuck. Every other resident of the Booster house had signed; the petition lacked only his signature to make it unanimous.

> Dear Mr. Anderson,
>
> We, the undersigned members of State's freshman football team, hereby protest the action of Coach Jim Sullivan in suspending Sean Reynolds, Bebop Leopoulos, Lonnie Akins, and Pete Pines from the squad.
>
> We further protest the demotion of several Booster athletes because of a few non-Booster players' efforts to break up the harmony of the squad. We feel that the above players have been treated unfairly. Unless they are reinstated immediately, we intend to drop out of football at State University.

"You guys sure you want to do this?" Fireball ventured when he had finished the second reading. "You sure you want to go this far?"

"We signed it, didn't we?" Leopoulos said irritably.

"Yeah, but it's pretty drastic."

"Not if we stick together. Come on, sign it! We're going to take it down to Anderson tonight."

"What if he doesn't support you?"

"What else *can* he do?" Reynolds demanded. "Without us, State'll have no team. Anyway, you see these letters? We're also giving a copy to every one of our sponsors! Anderson will play ball when those guys get on the phone and start calling him."

CHAPTER 14

It's an Order

SEAN REYNOLDS was right! Five minutes after Biz Anderson received the petition, he was on the phone trying to locate Nik Nelson and Jim Sullivan. But, for once, Anderson was outwitted. Nelson and Sullivan weren't at home, and they didn't go home until late. The next day, they kept away from the phone and the office until just before practice when they jumped into their warm-ups and rushed onto the field.

Anderson didn't have a chance to talk to them until after Thursday's workout. By that time he had worked himself into a cold fury, figuring that the two coaches were giving him the runaround. He went right out to the practice, sat stubbornly in the bleachers until practice was over, and then cut out onto the field.

"You two trying to avoid me?"

Nelson turned around in surprise. "Why, no, Mr. Anderson," he said slowly. "Of course not. What's on your mind?"

IT'S AN ORDER

"Plenty! What's this I hear about Akins, Reynolds, Leopoulos, and Pines? My phone's been ringing incessantly! My Booster friends are calling me and asking what's going on. I also have a petition here signed by everyone in the Booster house. What was the reason for your hastiness, Sullivan?" He turned angrily on the towering line coach. "Suppose you tell me what it's all about."

Sullivan cleared his throat nervously. "It boils down to a matter of discipline, Mr. Anderson. I sent those four to the showers because they failed to follow coaching instructions."

"I'd think you'd have displayed more leadership, Sullivan. I can't understand a grown man losing his head when he's supposed to be a teacher. Anyway, I want those boys reinstated. Immediately! We can't have trouble with the team in the middle of the season."

"Those players were wrong, Mr. Anderson," Sullivan said mildly. "They were sullen and wholly uncooperative."

"Why?"

"I suppose because we gave the team a little shake-up."

"Whose idea was that?"

"It was mine, Mr. Anderson," Nelson said quickly. "Jim's right. Some of those players have been impossible. They won't work, and they've got some of the others following the same pattern."

"What about the troublemakers? Hilton and Cohen and the rest of that group from Valley Falls?"

"They're not troublemakers, Mr. Anderson. Just the opposite. They've made some of the Booster guys look like high school freshman players. We just had to move them up to the first string."

"And you broke up a great team."

"I don't think so," Nelson protested. "In fact, I think

the way the team shapes up right now, it's as good or better than the varsity."

"That's impossible. Finley's out of position, and you've benched four of the best players on the squad. I dislike the necessity of saying this, but I think a lot of this is Rockwell's doing. He coached those Valley Falls kids, didn't he?"

Nelson nodded. "Yes, he did. But he's never said a word about any of them to me. Ever say anything to you, Jim?"

"Never!"

"Well, be that as it may, those four association boys have to be reinstated."

Sullivan shook his head stubbornly. "I'm sorry, Mr. Anderson," he said firmly, "but if those boys are reinstated without making some sort of an apology, you'll have to accept my resignation."

"It's accepted," Anderson snapped back.

Sullivan turned and walked away without another word. There was a dead stillness as Nelson shuffled his feet uncertainly and watched his friend stride swiftly away. Anderson broke the silence.

"Nelson, I want those suspended players to make this trip, and I want all of them back in their old positions."

"But what about these others? Hilton and Cohen and—"

"I thought we discussed them before! I thought we were trying to discourage them."

"They're not the type who discourage very easily," Nelson said grimly.

"Well, then, cut them from the squad."

"I wouldn't feel right about that, Mr. Anderson."

"What if you're ordered to cut them?"

IT'S AN ORDER

Nelson sucked the air deep into his lungs. "If you say to do that, Mr. Anderson," he said in a strained voice, "I'll do it, of course."

Anderson turned on his heel. "All right," he said harshly. "It's an order!"

Nik Nelson had never faced a task as difficult or as unpleasant as the one before him the next afternoon. He dressed slowly and reluctantly, trying to figure how he could soften the blow. All year he had leaned on Sullivan's shoulder when presented with a tough situation. Now he had to go it alone.

There wasn't much life in Nelson's voice when he called the squad together at the end of the light workout and shocked them with the announcement he had been dreading all day. His words were spoken so softly that the players had to strain to hear them.

"I've got to do something right now that I sure dislike. I have to cut the squad! This is going to hurt. Hurt a lot of you players who deserve a better break.

"Because of certain coaching and . . . and . . . other requirements, I have been advised that the squad is to be limited to twenty-two players. The list is posted on the bulletin board. I realize that a lot of you play football because you love the game, but I've got to follow orders."

There was an awkward silence, and then Nelson continued. "All of you who are dropping out are eligible for the dorm teams, of course, and . . . well, it's my hope that you will keep in shape.

"Everybody who plays football does it primarily because he loves the contact, the hard knocks, the good fellowship, and the hard fight for a job, and . . . well, I guess most of you have heard me talk about the hard way. Maybe this cut will be just another test for you along the line of the hard way. Anyway, if I can ever help you . . . well, all you have to do is let me know."

It was more than awkward. Even the Booster stars felt the tension and depression evident in Nelson's voice and attitude. They knew they were all set, of course. Still, there was a little twist of apprehension in their hearts as they headed for the locker room.

Chip's heart was trying to push its way up through his throat. For once, even Soapy was left completely speechless.

It was probably psychological. At any rate, no one hurried to check the list of names posted so conspicuously on the bulletin board in the team room. However, after his shower and after he had dressed, each player sauntered past the board and gave it a perfunctory glance. Only it wasn't a perfunctory inspection. It was a desperate examination, backed up by a little prayer and all the hopes and dreams and the hard work of training camp and three weeks of daily practice on the campus.

The names were listed alphabetically, but that was small help. It simply speeded the heartbreak for athletes like Chip, Biggie, Soapy, Red, Speed, Alonzo Patterson, Kip Waldorf, Donnell Wells, Kirk Powell, Hector Garcia, and Dave English.

Chip's heart sank to his shoes. All along he'd guessed what the posting held. Now he knew for sure. There wasn't anything to be said. He and all his Valley Falls friends had been cut. Though he had given the board only a cursory glance, he knew almost name for name the players who had been kept on the squad. The Booster stars were all there! And Eddie Anderson's name was there too. Just as he had known it would be.

It was bitter to swallow, but Chip and the others took it. Took it without a word. Except for Soapy. The irrepressible Soapy was hurt, and his words bitter.

"Keep in shape! Humph! What for? What a joke! Well, I've learned my lesson. No more football for me!"

Chip stopped Soapy's pity party. "Oh, yes, there is!" he said. "We're going to play for Jeff! All of us! We're not quitting!"

"You think Rock will hold still for this?" Schwartz asked, his voice choking with frustration.

"Of course not!" Morris retorted fiercely. "It's a dirty deal!"

"Don't let it get you," Cohen advised. "Politics won't keep us down next year. Personally, I'd just as soon spend this year studying and playing with the dorm team. Things will be different next year. Wait and see."

"Right!" Chip added, with more enthusiasm than he felt.

"Maybe Rock will do something about it," Soapy said hopefully.

"He's never let us down yet," Chip assured his roommate. "When the proper time comes, he'll be there!"

Chip didn't say all the things he was thinking. He knew there was something bigger than a clash of personalities involved here. It was a principle that was being brought out into the open, and Chip knew that Rock would be on the right side in that controversy. "Look," he said, summing it up, "we'll keep our mouths shut and we'll take it and we'll show the guys at Jeff that we're with them."

"It isn't fair," Schwartz persisted. "How about Eddie Anderson? Why wasn't he cut?"

Speed Morris answered that in a flash. "Because he's Mr. Big's son, that's why! He doesn't even know an end zone from an end run."

"Maybe not, Speed," Chip agreed patiently, "but Eddie's a good guy, and if he's been lucky enough to make the squad, more power to him. That's none of our business."

"I'll bet his old man made it some of *his* business," Speed retorted.

Speed Morris and Red Schwartz would have been amazed if they could have heard Eddie Anderson at that instant. Eddie was talking to Nik Nelson in the coaches' office, and what he had to say didn't take much time.

"Good luck, Coach. I guess you've got a lot on your mind without worrying about me. I hope you'll understand when I say that I appreciate your position. I just happen to know that half a dozen of the players who were cut are so much better than I am that the comparison is silly. I wouldn't feel right." He held out his hand. "Thanks for all the time you spent on me. Good-bye."

Eddie headed straight for the business office. Luck was with him, and he got in just as it was closing. Whatever he had to do didn't take much time. Thirty minutes later, he was home. As he packed his suitcase, Eddie steeled himself for what promised to be an extremely delicate dinner conversation with B. G. Anderson.

Downstairs, Eddie's father was reading the sports page of the *University Herald*. There was a pleased expression on his face as he read the list of names of the freshman athletes who would make the trip to York. Upstairs he could hear Eddie's stereo. He breathed a satisfied sigh and resumed his reading. In a few minutes he dropped the paper and relaxed. Eddie had survived the final cut. He'd come around. The youngster just needed to be needled a bit! One thing was definite—Eddie had a lot of his old man's fighting spirit.

He looked up when Eddie entered the room carrying his backpack and a suitcase. "Thought you were leaving for York in the morning. Has the game time changed? I'll drive you down to the sports complex to meet the bus."

"But I'm not going down to the sports complex, Dad. I'm going over to the dorms. I'm moving into Jeff. Furthermore, I've quit football!"

"Moving into Jeff? Quit football! What's the matter with you, son? Out of your mind?"

"No, I don't think so, Dad. I think I'm very much in my mind!"

"Why, I never heard such nonsense."

"It's not nonsense, Dad. It's good sense. I want to live a normal college life. I want to belong. I can't get into the swing of things living at home right on a school campus. I want to be with the guys, the right kind of guys."

"What's the matter with the guys at the Booster house?"

"I don't belong there. Besides, they're not my type."

"And you're going to find the right type at Jeff?"

"Yes, I am. They're right because they study, work, and play football. What's more, they think right."

"This is absurd! I won't permit it! I'll be a laughing-stock!"

Eddie stood up then. He was disappointed by his father's attitude but fully determined to go through with his plans. "I'm sorry, Dad. I'd hoped you'd support my view just once."

"Now, Eddie," Anderson said, rising to his feet, "you listen here. If you move out of this house and go any-where except the Booster house, your allowance is cut off as of that minute. Furthermore, I won't help with your college expenses."

"You won't need to, Dad. I have a job."

"A job! Where?"

"Grayson's."

"If you wanted a place like Grayson's, why didn't you say so? I'll buy you one! I'll buy you two of them!"

CHAPTER 15

Moving Out and Moving In

EDDIE ANDERSON dropped his suitcase on the floor with a bang and grinned good-naturedly at Biggie Cohen. Then he held out a blue slip of paper. "This says a guy by the name of Pete Randolph will give me a room."

Biggie eyed Anderson uncertainly. "A room? What for?"

"I'm moving in!"

"Moving in? You mean it?"

"Yep! Biz doesn't think I can get along on my own, and so I'm about to see how the other half lives."

"No!"

"Yes! Now, where's this Pete Randolph?"

Fifteen minutes later Eddie Anderson, Jeff's newest resident, closed the door of 306 and followed Biggie down to the first-floor lounge where they joined Speed and Red.

"Eddie just moved in," Biggie explained.

"Yep," Anderson added lightly. "I moved out! I took a job, and I've dropped out of freshman football."

"A job?" Schwartz repeated incredulously. "You crazy?"

"Dropped out of football?" Speed echoed. "You *must* be nuts! You were in solid—in like Flint, or, at this place, in just like Finley!"

"That's the reason I dropped out!"

Joel Ohlsen began rapping on the speaker's table in the front of the room just then, giving Speed and Red time to figure out that cryptic remark.

"Hey, everybody," Ohlsen said loudly, "give me your ears for a—"

"Ears! He wants our ears!"

"I *need* mine!"

"Listen up, guys," Ohlsen pleaded. "Give me your attention. I've been asked to make an announcement. The student council guy will be here in a couple minutes for the elections, and there's something you ought to know.

"Now listen! Some of you may not know that Chip Hilton and Biggie Cohen and Red Schwartz and Soapy Smith and Speed Morris dropped out of freshman football this afternoon, and a couple of us have figured out that's the best news we've had since we moved into Jeff. It means we're going to win the dorm championship!"

Ohlsen didn't have a chance to continue because the room erupted. Joel raised his hands and finally there was silence again.

"Now, while we're waiting, Hal Kenney will tell you the rest of it. Everybody knows Hal. He's the guy who's been practicing the clarinet every morning!"

Kenney joined Ohlsen and waited, smiling, until the boos ceased. "I don't know why Joel asked me to do this, but here goes! A bunch of us on the first floor have been talking about the dorm election, and we'd like to suggest that we elect Chip Hilton unanimously to the presidency of Jeff. What d'ya say?"

There wasn't any question about the popularity of Kenney's suggestion. Everybody in the room was on his feet cheering when the student council representative arrived. Brett Lindsay was just a bit surprised, but he held steadfastly to his pace and made his way up the aisle. He tapped the table for attention and called the meeting to order.

"The chair will now accept nominations for the presidency of Jefferson Hall."

Joel Ohlsen rose to his feet and was recognized. Joel said distinctly and proudly, "We have one candidate. I should like to present the name of William 'Chip' Hilton for the office of president of Jefferson Hall."

Lindsay was obviously surprised. "*One* candidate? That's strange. Of course, I shall have to call for other nominations. Is there a second to the nomination before the chair?"

"I second the nomination," Tug Rankin said quickly.

"Are there any other nominations?" Lindsay called patiently. "If not, I shall entertain a motion that the nominations be closed."

"I so move," Hal Kenney said.

"Second the motion," Caleb Shepherd added.

Lindsay then called for a standing vote. One quick glance was sufficient to confirm to the precise chairman that it was a unanimous choice, and the election of the other officers followed quickly. A few moments later, Lindsay departed, turning the meeting over to Bull Warner, the new vice president.

Warner called for the other officers to join him and presented each in order. Joel Ohlsen had been elected treasurer, and Red Schwartz brought down the house with his commendation: "Joel has more money than Bill Gates."

Speed Morris was elected secretary, and Biggie Cohen won an overwhelming victory as sergeant-at-arms. And it was Cohen who suggested the Jeffs all reassemble at 11:15 to welcome their new president when he came home from work.

Two hours later Chip and Soapy had barely reached the porch when Biggie pounced and ushered them into the jammed lounge.

"Greetings, Mr. President!"

"Speech! Speech!"

"What's *this* all about?" Chip asked.

"Yeah," Soapy demanded. "Let's have an explanation!"

Fifty voices gave Soapy the explanation, and then it was all Biggie could do to keep Soapy from making a speech. But he quieted down when Chip thanked the boisterous crowd for its confidence in him.

"I'll try to be a good president for you," he promised.

"What's the first bit of business on the agenda?" someone shouted.

Chip grinned. "Football business!" he replied decisively.

"Football business?"

"That's right! Right now! I want the guys who've been playing for Jeff and any newcomers to remain right here."

"Where you gonna practice?"

"Right here, right now! We'll have a nuts and bolts practice for thirty minutes, and then we'll do some studying. Another thing. I want every player on the squad out in front of Jeff in the morning at 6:30 sharp! We're going to do a little work. Soapy, dig up some computer paper and tomorrow we'll need a big dry-erase board."

Soapy's mouth fell open and he gazed at Chip incredulously. "A dry-erase board! Where? Where am I gonna get one of those?"

"You'll find one somewhere. We'll need fresh markers too. All right, now for the offense. We're going to use the

I-formation exclusively, but I've got to have something to draw it out on—"

"I can get a huge board in five minutes if you'll give me a couple of guys to help," said Eddie Anderson as he moved forward, grinning broadly. "You can put me down as a candidate for the team too."

Chip shook his head. "Hey, Eddie. Sorry, you're not eligible. Team's only open to Jeff residents. Besides, you're on the freshman team."

Anderson smiled again. "You're wrong on both counts, Mr. President. I do live in Jeff, for one, and, two, I dropped out of freshman football."

"You live here! Since when?"

"Since about 7:35 this evening. Come on, Biggie and Soapy. Let's go get the board."

Ten minutes later, the three were back. Chip called the Jeffs together and began his outline of the plays.

"We'll use the I-formation. It operates a lot like the T, except for the positioning of the fullback and halfbacks. The line is balanced, and the ends can float a bit or play tight, according to the situation. They're usually split though.

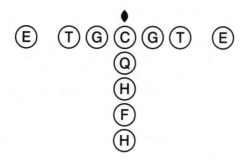

MOVING OUT AND MOVING IN

"We'll work on the best play in football, the off-tackle play. It runs on both sides, of course. I'll number the line to make the play easier to understand. Note how far the left guard has to move. He's got to be fast!

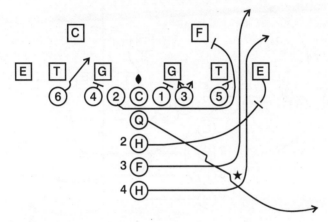

"I guess the line blocking is clear enough. The guard, 2, has to really move to get out ahead of the play and hit the linebacker, F. If the end, 5, is having trouble with the defensive tackle, T, his own tackle, 3, will have to help him out, and the right guard, 1, will have to take the defensive guard by himself. OK?

"The blocking by the backs is simple enough. Halfback, 2, takes the end, and the fullback, 3, is the personal blocker for the ball carrier, 4. The quarterback fakes as if he's kept the ball here at this star and keeps his hands hidden while he cuts back as if to pass. Lots of times he *will* keep the ball and run or pass. Maybe I'd better outline the pass right now. Got an eraser, Eddie?"

Anderson cleaned the board quickly, and Chip again placed the I-formation on the board. Then he explained each player's assignment for a pass play.

"This is a little tricky, but I guess we can handle it. The line blocking is simple enough with the exception of left guard, 2. He's got to pull out just as before, but circle back and block the defensive right end. Get it?

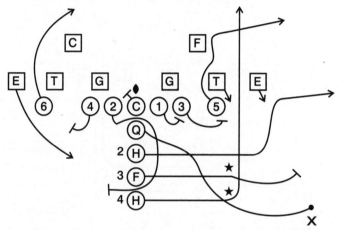

"There's four receivers: the ends, 5 and 6, breaking downfield, the halfback, 2, going out into the flat, and the left halfback, 4, driving over tackle and straight up the field.

"The fullback, 3, fakes to take a lateral at the first star and then goes on out to block. After faking the lateral to 3, the quarterback fakes again to 4 and keeps the ball. He tries to find an open receiver from position X.

"We'll use the regular 6-2-2-1 or the 5-3-3 or seven-box or a seven-diamond defense, depending on what's called in the defensive huddle."

Chip paused and then made a quick decision. Immediately, he began to sketch a defense on the board.

"This is called the 'umbrella' pass defense. We'll use it when our opponents are almost certain to pass. It's designed to prevent touchdown passes and assumes that

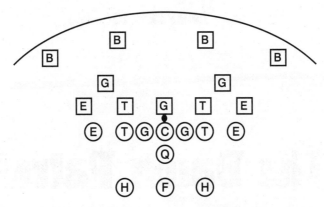

short passes may click once in a while. I've set it up against a T-formation just for purposes of illustration, but we'll use it against any attacking offensive formation."

Chip drew a line above the last line of defense and explained that the distribution of the backs gave the impression of an umbrella. Then he called it a day, saying, "All right, guys. That's enough for tonight."

Later, as Chip and his friends took the elevator up to the third floor and sat in Eddie's single room, the conversation switched back to football.

"You're sure taking this dorm football seriously, Chip," Anderson said pointedly. "What's the big deal? It wouldn't be because the dorm champs play the freshmen on Saturday, November 12, would it?"

Chip grinned. "Could be," he said, looking sideways at Anderson. He winked gravely. "It could be!"

CHAPTER 16

The Dawn Patrol

THAT THUMP was unmistakable! Curly Ralston stopped abruptly and lifted his eyes to look above the bleachers. Sure enough, it was a football. Ralston's experienced eyes calculated the flight of the spiraling ball, and he mentally registered sixty yards. His curiosity aroused, Ralston turned and retraced his steps, glancing at his watch at the same time. "Hmmm," he mused. "Unbelievable."

The sight that met his eyes through the high, wire gate was unbelievable too. There, running down punts, silently and almost viciously, it seemed, was a group of State students in jeans, sweat shirts, and cleats. And they ran, blocked, and tackled with complete abandon, despite the absence of pads. Ralston had known lots of kids who were so enthused about football that they practiced at dawn or even at midnight. And, despite the inconveniences, they had all expressed their love of the game with hilarious shouts and exulting cries of sheer joy.

But there was nothing spirited here. These students were practicing grimly, purposefully, and silently. Ralston shifted his glance to the kicker. He knew that long-legged kid, all right. That was Hilton, Rockwell's protégé. Some of the others looked familiar too. He turned away and continued his restless morning jog. But he couldn't get those kids out of his mind even though this early morning run came at the end of a sleepless night caused by his varsity problems. He resolved to ask Nik Nelson about it on Monday. Then he was struck by another thought. The freshmen were playing at York. "How come Hilton didn't make the trip?" he muttered.

Ralston thought about turning back, but then the impact of his varsity problems struck home again, and he shrugged his shoulders and continued. He was thankful that his inexperienced squad had an open day. The varsity needed a rest. "Three games and two losses," he breathed. "And four tough ones to go! I sure wish *this* year was over!"

When the big clock on the Student Union tower chimed seven o'clock, Chip's dawn patrol headed for the dorm and the showers. The dorm teammates trudged along in groups of two or three, talking softly as if they thought the normal pitch of their voices might awaken someone.

At two o'clock that afternoon, the dawn patrol was back at Alumni Field, dressed this time in the regulation dorm football uniforms. Chip recognized several familiar faces in the Garfield Hall lineup. Donnell Wells and Kirk Powell were there, grinning and promising a severe stomping, but Chip wasn't worried. He knew they were kidding, but he knew, too, that except for two or three spots he had a team that compared favorably with the freshman first string. Only one detail really worried him. That was the football condition of Bull Warner and Tug

Rankin. Chip and his brother Jeffs had persuaded the two heavyweights to help them win the dorm championship—for a number of important reasons!

Joel Ohlsen was there in a uniform several sizes too small for him and, sick or not, prepared to play if he was needed. Chip had backed Warner up with Caleb Shepherd, and Adam Russo with Moses Jackson.

On paper, Chip figured it was a good team. The starting lineup placed Schwartz and Soapy at the ends, Biggie and Adam at the tackles, Kip and Eddie at the guards, and Dave at center. Chip was at quarterback and Speed and Tug were at the halfback positions, with Bull at fullback. It was a big, speedy team, practically the reserves, except for three positions. Garfield never had a chance. The game turned into a rout! Jefferson, substituting liberally, won easily, 42-9. Chip kicked six consecutive extra points.

In the bleachers, Jim Sullivan sat beside Dad Young and told him why he wasn't in York with the freshman team. Sullivan and the director of athletics were flanked by Henry Rockwell and Dr. Mike Terring, State's team doctor.

"I have a spot for you in the Physical Education Department," Young assured Sullivan. "You'll be better off in the long run."

Sullivan grinned. "I won't have the mental stress," he said thankfully. "That's for sure!"

Rockwell listened to the conversation without a word, poker-faced and grim. When Sullivan repeated Anderson's reference to the Valley Falls players, Rock's jaw muscles tightened a bit, but there was no other indication that he was interested.

Dr. Terring, sitting beside Dad Young, took it all in too. Terring was built like a standing guard. His shoulders were broad, and he gave the impression of great physical strength. His voice added to the general effect, for he spoke crisply and confined his opinions to few words. But it was all deceptive. The popular physician had never played football, and the rough exterior housed a warm and friendly spirit. He and Dad Young were close friends and that may have accounted for his particular interest in State's athletic teams, especially football. Terring had an extensive practice, but somehow he found time to be available for all the athletes too.

Fiercely loyal to Dad Young and the veteran director's athletic principles, Terring listened to the discussion with keen interest. But he didn't permit the conversation to distract him from the dorm game. He watched the first quarter in silence, but as Chip and his Jeffs continued to dominate the fiercely fought battle, he moved over beside Rockwell.

"Maybe I'm crazy, or perhaps it's the quality of the opposition," he said admiringly, "but I think that Jeff quarterback is better than anything Coach Ralston's got on the varsity. How come he isn't out for the team?"

"He's a freshman," Rockwell said briefly.

"Oh, you know him?"

"He ought to," Sullivan interrupted. "He coached him for four years."

"Why isn't he playing freshman ball? He's good!"

"He's more than that," Sullivan added. Then he turned to Rockwell. "I'm not saying this because you're here, Coach, but that kid is the best all-around back I ever saw. He can do everything!"

"You're dead right!" Rockwell said grimly.

Terring was confused. "I still don't understand why he isn't playing freshman ball. Grades a problem?"

"His grades are very good. It's because he hasn't got a Booster for one reason," Sullivan said bitterly. "And because he showed up B. G. Anderson's personal ball of fire for another."

"You mean they pass up a player like that just because he hasn't got a Booster behind him?" Terring demanded incredulously. "Why, it's impossible!"

"Not so impossible," Young said. "Not when Biz Anderson's running the show. I have a hunch he's riding for a fall though. Prexy's just biding his time."

"You mean President Babcock?"

"Right. Prexy's just waiting for this Booster bubble to cause some sort of trouble. Then Biz Anderson will dance to a different tune."

That night Chip Hilton danced to a different tune too—and with Mitzi Savrill!

Yes, Chip danced his first dance with Mitzi Savrill. One evening he had stopped to look at the couples in one of the Fine Arts dance rooms and, without knowing exactly why, he walked in. He talked a few seconds to the instructor and was practicing dance steps minutes later with an extremely patient young coed. That was the first of several quick lessons. When Soapy asked him to go to the dance Saturday night at the Student Union to see if Eddie had been kidding about Mitzi, Chip surprised Soapy with his answer. "Sure let's go."

Eddie hadn't been kidding. He was there with Mitzi, and Soapy immediately cut in. Eddie joined Chip.

"Hear the freshman score? Tied 12-12. Guess they could have used one of those six kicks you knocked down this afternoon. Bet Nelson's boiling."

"York's tough," Chip commented. "They've won four straight!"

Eddie changed the subject. "How about a dance with Mitzi? We can't let her be bothered by Soapy all evening, can we?"

Chip swallowed hard. "Of course not. I'll wait for the next slow one. That is, if Mitzi doesn't mind."

"Mind? Stop kidding! You don't talk to girls much, do you?"

"*Me?*"

"Yes, you! Anyway, the next dance is coming up—a slow one, and it's yours."

Chip's heart was thumping as it did before the opening kickoff of every game when he followed Mitzi through the crowd to the edge of the floor. He put his arms around her and held her as if he were afraid she would break.

Chip knew they were dancing because they were moving, but he had no sense of the rhythm or timing the instructor had said he had in the dance room. He felt as if every person on the floor was watching them. He wished the music would stop or that there would be a power failure in the Student Union. The perspiration began to flow, and he was completely flustered, bumping into almost everyone unfortunate enough to get in their path.

Chip froze! He felt as if he were walking through a waist-high snowdrift and he began to pray that the band would hurry up and finish the song. He vowed he'd never let himself get trapped into dancing again. This wasn't fun! This was torture! What fun could anyone see in this stuff?

Then Mitzi lifted her big, violet-blue eyes to his face and said, "Oh, Chip, you're a wonderful dancer. And you told me you couldn't dance! I love to slow dance, and you've got to promise me right now to dance every one of them just with me. Promise?"

Chip never knew why he nodded. But he did! Nodded and returned her smile, and suddenly and inexplicably, for the first time, he caught the beat of the music and found himself following the rhythmic flow as easily as if he had been dancing all his life. Chip felt Mitzi respond with the swaying of her body and the sliding of her feet and sensed that they were dancing in perfect harmony, as one person.

Soapy had surrendered Mitzi to Chip with an incredulous look and watched with disbelieving eyes as Chip began to dance. "I don't believe it," he gasped. "Eddie, I've known Chip Hilton all my life and I've never seen him dance."

"Never underestimate the power of a woman, Soapy," Eddie chided. "Especially Mitzi Savrill."

College life moved swiftly for Chip after that Saturday night. Studying, classes, dorm football, work, and his duties as a freshman class officer and the dorm president barely left time for E-mails to his mom and old high school friends in other universities. He seldom saw any of the Booster players.

The Saturday football trips had interfered with Fireball Finley's progress with Mitzi, since Saturday afternoon football and dances at the Student Union were the only social luxuries her busy life permitted. Surprisingly, Chip didn't miss freshman football at all. He tried to analyze it but could only figure it was because of his interest in the Jeff team and the possibility of winning the dorm championship.

Saturday, October 29, rolled around before he realized it was possible, and Chip led Jeff to an easy 38-13 victory over Carnegie Hall that morning on Alumni Field. That same afternoon, the varsity dropped a close one to Wesleyan by a score of 20-19. It was Curly Ralston's third loss of the season. To make it worse, the freshman team lost its first game of the season that same afternoon at Midland Junior College by one point with a 13-12 score.

Most of the freshman stars took the loss philosophically. But not Fireball Finley! Coming back on the bus that night, Fireball was bitter and angry.

"We deserved to lose today. You guys have missed too many practices, and you're dogging it."

"What's the harm if we miss a day or two? Besides, it's only one game. We've been practicin' since August," moaned Bebop.

"It isn't right. Besides, Nelson's getting wise. He'll send Dr. Terring up here right off the bat. Terring's no fool! He's going to figure out you're pulling a fast one; and then someday one of us will really be sick, and he'll think we're faking."

"Oh, that country doctor couldn't catch a cold. Anyway, how can any doctor tell whether a guy really has a sprain or a stomachache or something like that? When I'm feeling like it, I'm staying home," Sean Reynolds barked.

That conversation seemed to represent the attitude of most of the stars. Their positions on the team were secure; their education, room, meal plans, laundry expenses, and spending money were assured, so why worry?

Bill Bell, the *Herald's* sports editor, really had a lot of football to write about in his column the next morning. And Chip Hilton's name was prominently mentioned in the veteran's column for the first time in the young athlete's college career. Eddie Anderson rushed into Chip's room early Sunday morning and pulled the bewildered quarterback out of bed.

"Look, Chip," he cried excitedly, "you made Bill Bell's sports column! Read it!"

FRESHMAN QUARTERBACK

THE FOOT IN FOOTBALL
By Bill Bell

The disastrous double loss by State's football forces yesterday afternoon focuses attention on the importance of the foot in football.

The freshman loss to Midland because of two missed extra points and a bungled field goal opportunity from the 10-yard line attest to the young squad's very evident kicking weakness.

The loss of greater importance, that of the varsity to Wesleyan, 20-19, all too clearly points to that same deficiency.

Coach Curly Ralston has been working since the first week in training camp to correct this glaring weakness, but to no avail. Wesleyan's margin of victory is reflected in the fact that they *made* two of their three kicks. State *missed* two of their three opportunities.

From the first game of the season, it was obvious that the freshman team would require extra *touchdowns* to compensate for the kicking weakness. In achieving their two wins, a tie, and one loss this season, the freshmen have made ten touchdowns and just two extra points.

And that brings me to a bit of information that may have far greater significance.

I received a letter last week from an old friend in Valley Falls. He wants to know why a freshman by the name of William "Chip" Hilton isn't good enough to make the freshman team. Chip Hilton, and here I quote, "played four years at Valley Falls High School, two years at end and two years at quarterback. The last two years he did all the punting, averaging a little over fifty yards, and was successful in thirty-four consecutive extra points. Besides, he kicked eight field goals ranging from fifteen to forty yards." There was more, considerably more, about his passing and running, but this excerpt should give you the idea of where I'm heading.

The name Hilton brought back fond memories, and I did some research. Sure enough, this freshman's father was the original "Chip" Hilton who earned all-American honors here at State University two decades ago.

Freshman Coach Nik Nelson confirmed Hilton had been dropped along with a number of other players to bring the new squad down to a size that the limited coaching staff could handle. Now, I could be wrong, but it seems to me there should be room on *any* squad—particularly *this* freshman squad—for a kicker of this caliber. Even if that team has been somewhat hastily described as a Wonder Team!

Suppose we save this material for the "to be continued" file until more information has been assembled. This column is all for advancing the game of football, but it's also old-fashioned enough to feel that there is still room for the foot in football. Always has been, always will be.

CHAPTER 17

Jubilant Jeffs

NEWSPAPER COLUMNISTS are careful not to risk plagiarism, and they check the contents of letters carefully before risking quotes. Mitzi Savrill knew the column she edited under the pen name of Birdie Byrd was considered a center for college gossip, and she was extremely careful about the contents and her sources. The day that Mitzi received an unsigned letter for publication, she deliberated a long time before deciding to use the letter in its entirety in *University Herald*.

> "The State Booster Association is attempting to dominate athletics and athletes here at State University. Note the recent dropping of eleven players from the freshman squad. Among whom were several who received all-state honors and who were good enough to fire the so-called reserves with sufficient fight to soundly trounce the so-called Wonder Team.

JUBILANT JEFFS

"Why were they dropped? Because not one of these freshmen was sponsored by a member of the Booster Association.

"Does this action mean that the university's athletic teams of the future will consist only of association players?

"And will all players except those who can present association 'membership' cards to the coaches be dropped?"

. . .

The "Jubilant Jeffs" refer to their player-coach, Chip Hilton, as "Mr. Toe." Hilton certainly deserves the name. Since Chip has been playing for Jeff, they have snowed under Garfield and Carnegie with Hilton kicking eleven consecutive points after touchdowns and one field goal from the thirty-four-yard line.

There's sure to be a big crowd next Friday afternoon at Alumni Field to see Jeff and Wilson, both undefeated, battle it out for the dorm league championship and the right to meet the freshman team on Saturday, November 12.

The championship battle between Jeff and Wilson received more publicity than the upcoming freshman game with Waynesburg Community College. It was natural for the involved dorm residents to talk about the dorm title game, but it was unusual for the rest of the student body and faculty to show so much interest. For some strange reason, *The Statesman* and *The Herald* played up the game all week. And they pulled no punches in referring to the Booster Association. Eddie Anderson and Soapy Smith seemed to enjoy it more than anyone else, just as if they were responsible in some way. But other readers' reactions differed, particularly in Anderson House.

"What's with these writers anyway?" Pete Pines demanded. "What do they want from us? We lose one game, and you'd think we committed the most heinous of crimes. Those scribblers make me sick!"

"Yeah, and how about the ink these dorm clowns get?" Leopoulos griped. "You'd think they were playing for the national championship."

Lonnie Akins put his finger on their real hate. "Everywhere that Hilton goes, he gets a good write-up in the papers. You see the story that Birdie Byrd wrote when he made freshman vice president? And when he got elected president of Jeff, you'd have thought he was the only guy to get a vote."

"Maybe Hilton writes that Birdie Byrd stuff himself," Finley joked. Then he continued seriously. "You guys been following Bill Bell's column? Hilton's dad must've been a real star. No wonder the guy's trying so hard. If I had a history like that, I'd be doing the same thing!"

"You seem to be doing all right," Sean Reynolds said. "You beat him out for quarterback, didn't you?"

"Maybe I did and maybe I didn't," Finley replied cryptically. "Maybe someone did it for me."

"You mean Biz Anderson?" someone asked.

"Yes," Fireball replied, "that's exactly who I mean, and I'm not too sure I like it. If I'm not good enough to be the number-one quarterback on my own, I don't want any help."

"That vehicle and the allowance and the clothes don't help?" Sean needled. "Not much they don't! I don't see you sending any of it back."

JUBILANT JEFFS

"You might be surprised," Finley said shortly as he walked toward the door. "Personally, I think you guys are in for a lot of surprises at this university unless you wake up and start to play ball." The slam of the door eliminated any comeback, and the room was quiet for a few seconds until the astonishment wore off. Then resentment took over.

"Who does he think he is?" Pines demanded. "What makes him think he's any different from the rest of us?"

"He's just mad because he isn't getting the raves Hilton's getting in the papers," Reynolds sneered.

Joe Maxim surprised everyone then. The big Polish tackle seldom joined in any conversation and spent most of his time studying. "Hilton's all right," he growled. "He's good! You know something else? I think Hilton has it all over Fireball when it comes to kicking, running, and playing quarterback. Another thing! If Hilton had been playing on this team—which he should be—we wouldn't have lost that game Saturday. Good night!"

There wasn't much talking after Maxim left. Every player on the freshman team respected Silent Joe. At six feet two and 210 pounds, he was in on every play, battling for every inch. And he played as hard in a scrimmage as he did in a game.

The next afternoon at practice, Nik Nelson noted that something new had been added to the stars' excuse list. Previously it had been bruises, aches, and simple strains. Now it was sore throats, colds, headaches, upset stomachs, and burning fevers. Anything that would suffice as an excuse for sleeping. A third of the squad was absent from practice, and Nelson headed directly for the phone afterward to call Dr. Terring.

"Hi, Doc. It's Nik Nelson. Are you too busy to visit Anderson House? I don't think there's anything wrong

with them except swelled heads and chronic laziness. . . .
I sure appreciate it, Doc. Will you call me at home? . . .
Thanks."

Doctor Terring didn't spend much time at 3646
Academy Avenue. When he left, there was a grimness
around his thin-lipped mouth and a purpose in his stride,
indicating strong emotion. Mike Terring didn't like lies.
Little lies, medium lies, or big lies. And he particularly
disliked lies about affected sickness. But he hadn't let on
during his examinations. He had simply made a list of
the complaints. All that time he was doing a lot of thinking. And not all his thinking was about spoiled athletes.

Friday afternoon, Dr. Terring was sitting in the
bleachers at Alumni Field beside Dad Young and Jim
Sullivan. Terring was an interested, quiet, intent, and
absorbed spectator.

Down on the field, Chip was having himself a day.
The Wilson team was big, aggressive, and strong. But
they hadn't faced a passer of Chip's skill and wit. Indeed,
that could very well have been said of the freshman
team, even the varsity. Chip threw long ones, short ones,
fed them into the flat, used his jump basketball toss over
the line, and lateraled the ball all over the place. His
finesse with fake handoffs completely baffled the hard-
charging Wilson line. The game turned into a rout just as
the Carnegie and Garfield encounters had been. Jeff won
easily, 37-6. Won the campus championship as easily as
that!

All through the game, Dr. Terring had been etching
strange hieroglyphics and numbers on a notepad. He
aroused the curiosity of his two companions, but they
kept quiet until the end of the game.

"What's that?" Young asked, pointing to the strange
marks.

JUBILANT JEFFS

"About the best football player and the greatest performance I ever saw on a football field," Terring replied. "Listen to this! Hilton attempted thirty-four passes, connected on twenty-eight, and had one interception. His punts averaged fifty-seven yards, and he kicked four consecutive points after touchdowns.

"In addition, he made three field goals of twenty-three, thirty-seven, and thirty-nine yards. He got away for two long runs for touchdowns and tossed passes for two more. That's all!"

There was a lot of celebrating at Jeff that night and a lot of dorm football talk at Grayson's. But Chip and Soapy weren't interested; they were thinking about Petey Jackson and Speed's Mustang. They were going home that night! The first time since classes had started!

Petey pulled up at eleven o'clock, tired but happy to see his friends. After two big cups of coffee, he announced he was ready for the return trip. A few minutes later they were on their way to Valley Falls with Speed behind the wheel. Chip and Soapy rode in the back seat.

That was the reason they didn't see Waynesburg Community College beat the freshmen 14-13 Saturday morning on Alumni Field. The varsity lost that afternoon too. The less said about that 7-6 defeat the better.

The *Herald's* Bill Bell played up the dorm championship. The freshmen were almost eliminated from the sports page, but Bell sure spread the ink on the Jubilant Jeffs. He had really done his homework on the backgrounds of Jeff's personnel.

FRESHMAN QUARTERBACK

JEFF CINDERELLA KIDS
STEAL WONDER TEAM'S THUNDER
By Bill Bell

State's Dorm League proves the game of football can be played for fun. Jefferson Hall, this year's championship team, proves something else. It proves students can work, study, and still play an outstanding game. Seven of the eleven starters are working their way through college. And every player on the squad passed his mid-term exams with an average of 80 percent or better.

That's right. I checked it. The figures came straight from Dean Murray's office.

That's par for the course, and when it comes to football, the Cinderella Kids exemplify my idea of what the great game of football is all about. Fun, recreation, discipline, spirit, pride, and team play.

Why make a great fuss about so-called Wonder Teams that are subsidized to earn a profit, provide entertainment for the public at large, please alumni, and gain prestige for the school?

Why should students and State football enthusiasts cheer and applaud athletes who are not representative of the normal student body?

There was a lot more about the Jubilant Jeffs. It wasn't too surprising considering the respect with which *The Herald's* sports editor regarded Birdie Byrd. And when she was in someone's corner, that was enough for Bill Bell.

Dr. Terring was in Chip Hilton's corner, too, even though he was lost in the big crowd for Homecoming Weekend. The dorm champions-freshman game was the first contest of the day's football doubleheader.

JUBILANT JEFFS

Alumni Field was jammed, swarming with students and faculty. Old grads renewed friendships at their tailgate parties. And, of course, all the members of the Booster Association were present this bright, crisp Saturday morning. It amazed the Wonder Team sponsors to find almost every person in the place cheering for Jeff!

"I think they'll do it," Terring said, nudging Dad Young. "What do you think?"

"Right," Young agreed doubtfully.

Chip won the toss and elected to kick. Finley chose to defend the south goal, although there was no wind, no real point to the choice. Chip's kick was high and carried to the goal line where Finley gathered the ball in and started up field. He didn't get far. Eddie Anderson dropped him with a shoestring tackle on the twelve-yard line.

Then, on the first play, Finley fooled every grandstand quarterback, fan, and opponent in Alumni Field. He fooled Chip Hilton too. Finley, setting up between the center, Leopoulos, and his guard, Akins, called a complete surprise: a quick kick. Bebop snapped the ball directly into Roberts's waiting hands. Junior got it off beautifully. The ball kicked up dust at the midfield stripe fifteen yards behind Chip and lazily bounced, end over end, toward the Jeff goal. Chip and Speed tore after the elusive pigskin, but it was wasted effort. Reynolds, Pines, and Maxim were right on their heels to surround the bobbing ball. They gathered around it in a tight little knot until it came to rest on the five-yard line. Even the Jeff residents had to cheer that call. It was good, smart football and good for eighty-three precious yards.

Up in the stands, Dad Young shook his head forebodingly. "I think the freshmen are fired up, Mike," he said appraisingly. "This stacks up to be a grudge game."

It was a grudge game! Chip found that out on the first play. After faking to Speed and Bull, he darted back into the end zone to throw a pass. It seemed as though the freshmen rushers got there as soon as he did, burying him under a vicious pile of flailing arms and knees. Chip covered up as best he could, but some of the elbows and fists and knees found their marks. The referee dug into the pile and pulled Chip to his feet. It was a safety! The freshmen led, 2-0.

Chip shook it off and kicked from the twenty-yard line down to the freshman thirty. Finley took the ball and made it to Jeff's forty-five before Cohen smashed into him like a runaway truck. Fireball bounced up in the air, hung there a second, and then flew back like a snapped rubber band, landing on his back. The ball skidded out of his arms, and Eddie Anderson grunted gleefully as he dove headlong and coiled his body around the loose ball on the forty-yard line.

Biz Anderson, sitting smack in the middle of the Booster's section, couldn't smother the cheer that leaped from his throat. "Atta boy, Eddie! Atta—" He stopped and looked around half-ashamed, but he was as proud as a father had a right to be. No one seemed to notice and Anderson pounded his fist into his open palm and muttered under his breath, "Eddie, that's my boy!"

Dr. Terring was on his feet, lifting his voice in a cheer for Eddie Anderson. He hardly noticed that Dad Young was pounding him on the back.

"This could lead to bloodshed," Dad was shouting. "Man! What action!"

Down on the field, Chip had hurried the Jeffs into the huddle. "Come on. Hurry! The spread! Got it? Get loose, somebody. I'll find you! On three now. Let's go!"

Soapy got loose, got behind Rentler, and kept going. Chip faked twice and then hung the ball out on the line, right to the five-yard line. Soapy looked up at exactly the right second, pulled in the sailing prize, and in three quick strides crossed the goal line untouched. Seconds later, Chip's toe kissed the ball for the extra point and Jeff led, 7-2.

"How about that! How about that!" Terring shouted excitedly. "Did you see that?"

Young nodded happily. "I saw it," he assured Terring, trying to defend himself from Mike's wildly waving arms. "Take it easy."

The seven points were all Jeff needed, as it turned out, because of Chip's kicking and passing. The freshmen were better on the ground. They drove the Jeffs down the field time and again. But they couldn't penetrate Jeff's stout umbrella defense within those last ten yards. Jeff held them three times inside the five-yard line. On defense, the freshman forward line was charging furiously, fighting toward Chip on every play, smashing him to the ground whether he had the ball or not.

"I don't like it," Young repeated over and over. "The officials ought to slap a few penalties on them. They're going to hurt that boy!"

Dad Young was right. Midway in the last quarter, Jeff went into its spread again and clicked for three straight passes. With the ball on the freshman thirty, Chip tried a pass again but could find no receiver and decided to run. He swept around right end, nearly getting away, but was forced out of bounds on the fifteen. Then it happened!

Just as Chip slowed down and turned to toss the ball to the official, Pete Pines and Lonnie Akins hit him. Pines caught Chip right at his hip pads, but Akins's 195 pounds crashed full across the back of the knees. Chip felt an unbearable pain shoot up his legs and then blacked out. His helpless legs wouldn't support his weight and his body folded, falling heavily backward.

Doctor Terring didn't wait for the call. He knew Chip Hilton was badly hurt. He hurried down the aisle and pushed his way through the crowd. One glance was all he needed. "Get the stretcher!" he said sharply. "Carry him into the trainer's room."

Something went out of the Jeffs after that. Caleb Shepherd reported for Chip and did his best, but it wasn't enough. Chip's absence demoralized his teammates. The jubilant freshmen smothered Jeff's feeble attack and took over on the ten-yard line. From there, they marched straight down the field. This time there was no goal-line stand. Finley smashed across from the five-yard line on the last play of the game. It didn't matter that Fireball's kick was wide. The clock had run out, the game was over, and the freshmen were the victors, 8-7.

Just as soon as that last play was over, the Jeffs scurried for the trainer's room. The final score wasn't very important right then.

"How is he, Doc?" Cohen asked anxiously, peering through the door of the training room.

"I'm all right, Biggie," Chip called. "Come in!"

That did it! Despite Mike Terring's protests, they all barged through the door to surround a buddy who could barely refrain from wincing with pain as the harried physician immobilized his legs.

"How about it, Doc?" Soapy demanded. "Is he really all right?"

Terring grunted. "There are no bones broken, if that's what you're worrying about," he said testily. "Now, get out of here. We're taking him up to the medical center for a few tests and observation."

"But when can we see him?" Ohlsen persisted anxiously.

"You can come up this afternoon. Two o'clock. Now, beat it! All of you."

The Jeffs probably weren't missed in the overflow crowd at the stadium, but not a single member of the championship dorm team saw State beat Southeastern University 12-0 that afternoon. A couple of Jeffs slipped down the hall to check the score from time to time, but that was as far as they wandered from Chip's room in the medical center until the nurse ushered them out.

"You can come back tomorrow," she said, shooing them out the door. "Ten o'clock in the morning. Yes," she assured Soapy, "I'll be on duty."

Fireball Finley wasn't very happy that night, but he turned up at the Student Union. Mitzi Savrill had coolly informed him earlier in the week that she had a date with Eddie Anderson. He got a frigid reception when he tried to cut in too. Mitzi held on to Eddie's arm and sent the unhappy star on his way.

"If you don't mind, Eddie," Mitzi said, ignoring Fireball completely, "I'd prefer to dance with you." She placed her arm over his shoulder. "Besides," she added icily, "I don't care for poor sports. Dirty football never appealed to me."

Mitzi's remarks might have accounted in part for the conversation that took place at Anderson House later that night when Finley appeared, grousing and grumbling.

"My, you're home early, lover boy," Sean Reynolds needled. "Mitzi stand you up?"

"Nobody stood me up," Fireball said grimly. "But I think this is as good a time as any to tell you guys just where I stand. I've been thinking about a lot of things since the game this morning. Enough of you guys play dirty football to spoil this whole deal for me. I'm through! Through forever with your kind of football!"

"And I suppose you're through with Mr. Biz too?" Akins asked slyly.

Finley took a step in Lonnie's direction, his eyes drilling hard into those of the big guard. "That happens to be my business," he said slowly. "But since you're so interested, you might as well know that I think you and Pete clipped Hilton deliberately this afternoon when he was out of bounds. Just the way you did the other time. You listening, Pete? I said *deliberately*. And that's even worse than dirty football! From now on, you just take the long way around me as much as possible."

"They couldn't stop," Sean growled.

"That's a miserable, cowardly lie!" Fireball barked. "And you know it! It was dirty football, and I'm through with guys who play it that way."

Finley's face was white with anger. His eyes were narrowed to thin slits, and the deep frown line above his nose attested to his feelings.

"And I don't like you either, Akins," he said slowly, enunciating each word carefully. "You're a coward and a rotten sport, and if you want to do anything about it, there's plenty of room outside. That goes double for you, Pines. You, too, Reynolds!"

There were no takers. Akins shifted uneasily in his chair and looked down at his feet. After a dead silence, Fireball continued. "Another thing! On Monday, I'm moving out of this chump dump." He moved to the door and turned for one parting shot. "Some Wonder Team!"

CHAPTER 18

Cinderella Kids

EDDIE ANDERSON was actually enjoying his father's company just like old times! The occasional dinners together at home were something they both looked forward to now that Eddie was working and proving he could make a go of college on his own.

"You know, Dad, there was a different spirit on the Jeff team. We all played together and for one another. The Booster stars were always complaining, quarreling, and arguing about who got what and why they didn't get more. It's just been more fun this way."

Biz nodded. "You've been playing a lot better, Eddie. I didn't know you had it in you!"

"I like playing guard, Dad. Chip thought I should play guard because I love to block. You knew he was coaching us, didn't you? I'm a little small for the position but fast enough to lead the interference, and that helps our offense. Besides, I'm not really good enough to play in the backfield.

"I wish you felt differently about Chip, Dad. Everybody likes him and admires his spirit. You wouldn't believe all the things he can do with a football. Besides, he's a solid student and the president of Jeff. He's even got all of us studying. Most of us study in the library between classes and on our off days. Our goal is for Jeff dorm to win scholastic honors. That'll prove football players and guys who have to work can be good students as well as anyone else. Half of us in Jeff work part time somewhere. It's tough to keep up sometimes, but I've never been happier!"

"I know, Eddie," his father said gently. "I'm extremely proud of you, working and studying and playing dorm football. Nelson had you playing out of position all the time, didn't he?"

"That was my fault, Dad. I always thought I was a back, and I guess I was too stubborn and proud to consider any other position."

Biz Anderson grinned and playfully poked Eddie in the shoulder. "I guess you come by those qualities naturally enough," he said quietly.

"I know, Dad, genetics, but they aren't the best qualities after all. Besides, I don't want to be that kind of player. I want to play football because of the fun of playing. The kind of fun we're having at Jeff. Practices are called some mornings at six o'clock! And you know what? Every single one of us turns up. That's more than the Boosters can say! They were always trying to dodge the work and find some kind of excuse to skip practice."

"They *must* like football, Eddie. You're not trying to tell me they don't like football?"

"I think they like football, Dad, but they don't like to pay the price. They like the games and the crowds and the excitement and the cheering and the newspaper clippings and the student rallies, but that isn't all there is to football.

"If a player really loves football, he'll play at six in the morning for the sheer love of the game. You know what would happen if you called freshman football practice at six o'clock in the morning? You wouldn't have a player there!"

"Wouldn't that be a little silly? To practice at six in the morning?"

"It wouldn't be silly if they had to work and that was the only time they had to practice."

"You've got something there, son. You'll be over for dinner on Wednesday, won't you? We can talk some more then."

"Sure, Dad! That'll be great!"

Biz started, stopped, and stammered a bit but finally got his question out. "By the way, Eddie, how are you fixed for money?"

Eddie grinned widely and reached into his pocket. "Sure, Dad," he said, chuckling. "How much do you need this time?"

Father and son laughed together at the corny joke, and Eddie started for the door. As he walked out across the broad porch and down the steps, he was smiling cheerfully. He hadn't had this much fun at home since training camp began in the summer.

B. G. hadn't said anything about hitting the books or given Eddie any directives. Yes, his father was changing. He was trusting his son more. B. G. had listened with patience and understanding while Eddie explained that only the freshmen's dirty play had kept the Jeffs from winning. There was a new respect in his father's eyes, and the family dinners had again become a precious time for sharing and listening to family interests.

Eddie chuckled. "First thing you know," he murmured, "Dad will want me to ask Chip Hilton over to dinner."

At that moment Eddie saw the familiar red SUV parked in the driveway beside the house. "That's weird," Eddie said. "Wonder what's going on?"

There was no one in the vehicle, but a white envelope rested on the dash. Eddie reached in and picked it up. The envelope was addressed to Mr. B. G. Anderson. Eddie hesitated. He wasn't sure he wanted to be the messenger boy again. "No, I'll leave it."

He continued toward Grayson's, but he suddenly felt deflated, and all the spring was gone from his step. The SUV, letter, and thoughts of Fireball Finley overshadowed how happy he'd been a few minutes before.

Some time later Biz Anderson left the house. He stopped in surprise, then walked over to inspect the vehicle in the driveway. He found the note, but it was too dark to read, so he went back inside to read the contents with puzzled eyes.

> Dear Mr. Anderson,
>
> I am returning the SUV. I had no business taking it in the first place. Thanks very much anyway though.
>
> I've also decided to move out of Anderson House tomorrow and will try to get into one of the dorms. I am sure I'll be happier in a dorm.
>
> Since I will now have to work, I've decided to give up football for the rest of this year.
>
> I am grateful to you for everything you've done for me.
>
> Sincerely,
> Fred Finley

Five minutes later Anderson was on the phone, trying to locate Nik Nelson. A half-hour of phoning brought no results, and he was forced to call the Booster house and ask Fireball Finley to meet him.

The meeting didn't go well, for either of them. Fireball was adamant. He was going to move out of the Booster house and drop football, and that was all there was to it! Anderson could get nothing else out of him. But he did get Fireball to promise to remain in the Booster house until he had a job lined up. "That will give him time to think it over," Anderson reflected. "And give Nelson time to find out the trouble."

Anderson didn't think to call Dad Young's home, which is where he would have found Nelson. Nik, Henry Rockwell, Dad Young, Mike Terring, and Curly Ralston were talking football over their coffee in the library.

"Oh, Rock!" Mike smiled, "I've got good news for you! Hilton checked out OK. He'll be sore for a while. I sent him back to the dorm this afternoon."

"Too bad he got hurt," Young observed. "The Jeffs would have whipped them, Nik, if he hadn't."

"I've been wondering about Hilton," Ralston interrupted. "I never said anything to you about it, Nik, but I saw him practicing at Alumni Field one morning at six o'clock."

"He's the best football player in school, Coach," Nelson said simply.

"Then why isn't he playing for you? I meant to ask you about him a long time ago, but I've had some team worries of my own." He laughed shortly, and the others joined in sympathetically.

Dad Young edged forward in his chair. Here was the opening he had been waiting for, and he glanced pointedly at Rockwell and Terring as he began. "I've been wanting to talk to you about the freshman football situation, Curly. I've been anxious to explain the Booster Association and a lot of its implications."

Curly Ralston learned a lot that evening about the Booster Association and about B. G. Anderson. Nik Nelson listened in silence. Later, after Ralston, Nelson, and Rockwell left, Young and Terring continued the discussion.

"I've been thinking about something, Dad," Terring said thoughtfully. "Something that might bring this freshman football fiasco to a head."

"Like what?"

"Like giving those freshman invalids a good rest, a good excuse to miss the practice they seem to dislike so much."

Dad Young looked at Terring with suspicious eyes. "You're up to something," he probed. "What's on your mind?"

Mike Terring wasn't talking. He wasn't going to let his best friend get mixed up in this wild idea. The doctor had resented the malicious manhandling of Chip Hilton the previous afternoon. The plan, building in his mind for the past two weeks, had begun to crystallize. Dr. Mike Terring had decided to take a hand in State's football problems!

The following afternoon, Sondra Ruiz, Dr. Terring's physician assistant, couldn't understand why her boss waited so anxiously in his office after the last patient had left. When Nik Nelson called the office, she thought it odd that the doctor went off to the Booster house, chuckling. In fact, she was a little bit puzzled. Terring hurried away with a glint in his eyes and a grin, just as if he were seeing the first patient of his career.

Sean Reynolds gave Mike Terring the surprise of his life! It kept him in the Booster house until all of the stars had returned after practice. Then Terring gathered everyone into the living room. His face was solemn. Things had turned out to be more serious than anything his plans had called for. Sean Reynolds wasn't faking after all.

"As of now, this house is under quarantine. Reynolds has developed what I believe are the symptoms of meningitis. To be safe, it's necessary to confine him and all the rest of you until we can be absolutely certain. I'll alert the medical center and must instruct all of you to remain indoors until I give you the OK. I'll be back in the morning."

There was a shocked, intense silence as the impact of Terring's announcement sunk in. Then there was a barrage of words and complaints.

"Meningitis! What's that?"

"He's gonna keep us here just because Sean wants a little extra sleep?"

"C'mon! Let's go see the sleeping beauty!"

Reynolds looked up at his teammates with watery eyes. "I feel terrible," he moaned. "The doctor thinks I've got meningitis. My neck's so stiff I can't move it, and I'm burning up."

His worried teammates backed out into the hall and took their subdued gripes back downstairs.

"Thought you were moving, Fireball!" Lonnie Akins sneered. "Looks like you didn't move quick enough!"

The news raced through University and across the campus. Nik Nelson called Biz Anderson right away.

"Mr. Anderson? Nik Nelson. I didn't have a chance to see Finley today, but I don't think it's too important now. Dr. Terring has just quarantined the Booster house!

"About an hour ago. Reynolds sent word to practice that he didn't feel well, and I asked Terring to take a look at him. Terring just called. He said it could be as much as two or three weeks, depending on the lab results. He said no one could leave since they might have all been exposed. I guess we'll have to cancel the game. . . . I know, I know, Mr. Anderson. But what can I do? . . . Yes, sir. I'll tell him to call you right away."

Dr. Terring got Nik Nelson's message from the answering service, but Mike didn't worry much about calling. "Let him fret," Terring muttered to himself. "It'll do Biz Anderson a lot of good to worry about something important for a change."

Terring did call Dad Young. Mike told him about the quarantine and the excitement it was stirring up. "Imagine," he said, his voice filled with concern, "imagine the odds of picking up the symptoms of a contagious disease just when everyone's looking forward to the big game with Oxford. Dad, I've got an idea. It just hit me! A good one! Why not let the Jeff team play Oxford?

"No, honest, Dad. You think I'd do a thing like that? You know me better than that. Remember that oath all doctors take? We heal the sick; we don't make them sick. But don't you think the idea of Jeff playing Oxford is a good one?"

Dad Young shook his head skeptically as he hung up the phone and chortled to himself. "Anyway, I'm going to call Prexy."

Sean's condition remained unchanged on Wednesday according to Terring, and Nelson called Anderson.

"Doc says they can't be released for the Oxford game, Mr. Anderson. I started to do that, but I got a call from President Babcock. He said to let the championship dorm team play the game. Prexy said Jeff would be a good match for any—

"I know Oxford's undefeated, but that's what he said and I passed it on to the papers. Sure! Jeff's agreed, and they're practicing down here on Alumni Field right now! No, I didn't do it, Mr. Anderson. It was President Babcock's decision. He authorized it."

Anderson was angry. What if the Jeffs *did* beat Oxford? What if they merely put up a good game? Of course, it was a long shot, but . . .

"They'll get killed, Nelson!" Anderson shouted. "Killed! Oxford destroyed York, 63-6, and the best we could do against York was tie them 12-12 on our own field. And Oxford *murdered* Midland!"

It was a good thing Anderson couldn't read Nelson's thoughts. Nik was thinking that the reason the freshmen had lost to Midland was because Chip Hilton wasn't playing to do the kicking. But Nik was careful to play along with Anderson, to agree with him. Inside, Nelson was ecstatic! Hilton and the dorm team might do it! Oh, man! A lot of people would sure love that!

Anderson didn't stop with Nik Nelson. He called President Babcock but didn't get anywhere. Babcock wasn't too enthusiastic about the Booster Association, and Terring's and Young's calls had given him a head's up. He wasn't going to reverse his permission for Jefferson Hall to play, and Anderson's arguments were completely wasted.

"I think it's a grand idea," Babcock said enthusiastically. "Think of it! A bunch of dorm students with a student coach! Reminds me of my old glory days. Dean Murray and I think it's a fine thing. We're all for it! Incidentally, Murray tells me your son is on the team. Congratulations! By the way, Mr. Anderson, I'd like to attend your next Booster meeting. I'm getting a little concerned about our freshman athletic program. See you at the game."

The story was something fresh and new in campus sports, and the papers played it up in every issue. Bill

FRESHMAN QUARTERBACK

Bell gave the game space every evening, and Birdie Byrd devoted two straight columns to the event.

The Booster stars loved the sports pages. Especially when they made the columns. They weren't very enthusiastic about the press the Jeffs were getting, but they read the papers Eddie Anderson made sure were delivered promptly.

"What's the school thinking of?" Pete Pines demanded. "They'll be a disgrace."

Fireball Finley had been reserved that boring week, but he couldn't resist a retort to Pines's remark. "They didn't disgrace themselves against us," he said belligerently. "If you ask me, it was the other way around. At least they played clean football!"

No one challenged him, and Fireball went back into his shell. He was in the same mood the next afternoon when the disgruntled stars huddled in the living room to listen to the campus radio coverage of the Oxford game.

There wasn't much for the stars to cheer about, but that wasn't true of the crowd that overflowed Alumni Field. The unique football story had caught the imagination of fans all over town, and they were there to see the Jeffs in action.

Oxford received and marched right up the field for a quick touchdown and the extra point. A moment later, Chip took the kickoff and carried to his own forty. Speed slashed over right tackle and raced to the Oxford thirty-five. There Chip hit Schwartz on a look-in pass for five and then sent Warner bulling through the heart of the Oxford line for the first down. Another pass hit Schwartz, crossing in front of Oxford's outside linebacker for seven more. Then Chip sent Eddie Anderson scampering around left end on a guard-lateral play that brought the fans to their feet with one continuous cheer as Eddie raced for the touchdown. The boot was good, and the game was tied, 7-7.

Oxford was a high-scoring team with a varied attack, and the game was filled with action. Oxford had scored three times and kicked two extra points while Jeff had fashioned two touchdowns, two extra points, a field goal and a safety to make it Oxford 20, Jeff 19, with just two minutes left to play.

Back in the Booster house, Fireball shocked every star in the room when he began to cheer for the Jeffs. "Come on, you guys," he gritted, when the dorm held Oxford on downs and took over on the Jeff fifteen. "Come on. Start moving!"

The Jeffs didn't hear him, but they got moving. Chip was using the spread now, and it was clicking. Oxford finally went into a 4-3-4 umbrella pass defense in a desperate attempt to guard against a touchdown thrown over the defensive players' heads. But the defense couldn't stop Chip's short accurate passes, and Jeff marched straight down to the Oxford twenty. There the defense stiffened and held three consecutive times. Chip looked at the clock and called time. There was barely time for one more play.

"Kick it, Chip," Biggie said, putting his arm across Chip's shoulder. "You can do it!"

"It's up to you, guys," Chip told them, looking around the circle of tired faces. "It's a tough one against this wind. Maybe we ought to try one more pass."

"We've only got two seconds left," Rankin said. "We can't afford to gamble. Besides, that's not a tough kick for you!"

"He's right!" Joel Ohlsen agreed. "I've seen you make tougher ones."

Chip nodded. "All right, but give me a tight line. We'll need more time too. Right, Speed? On two, Adam! Everyone, be careful, stay clean—no penalties!"

FRESHMAN QUARTERBACK

The noise of the crowd completely died when Jeff lined up for the field-goal attempt, and the fans saw Chip make his spot in front of Speed's knee. In the Booster house, Chip's signals echoed in the stilled living room.

Fireball Finley bowed his head as he heard those numbers, and he whispered a little prayer for the rival he had plagued all season. Chip Hilton was a real football player. A guy who played football the right way. A guy who played because he loved the game.

The answer to Finley's prayer came suddenly and without doubt. Fireball knew the kick was good before the student announcer's voice could penetrate the thundering roar.

"It's good! It's good! What a kick! What a game!

"The Jubilant Jeffs, now the Cinderella Kids, have just handed Oxford their first defeat of the season! Is that a storybook finish or is that a storybook finish? Two seconds to play, behind by a single point, and Mr. Toe—Mr. Chip Hilton—knocks down a perfect placement from the twenty-eight-yard line. That ball had to carry thirty-eight yards in the air, State fans, against the wind.

"Here's more good news on the Cinderella Kids, and right off the gridiron. Coach Nik Nelson just told me that this same Jeff team will start against A. & M. Thanksgiving morning."

CHAPTER 19

Their Own Two Feet

DR. MIKE TERRING was in good spirits for a physician who was facing a potential outbreak of meningitis. The Booster players had seen him coming as he pulled in the driveway and now greeted him sullenly.

"Hey, Doc, how much longer you gonna keep us penned up here?" Bebop Leopoulos demanded.

"That depends on Sean's condition," Terring said calmly. "We have to be cautious. But I'm beginning to believe now, after his latest lab work came back, that he may have had the flu, which resembles the symptoms. I'll know better after I have a look at him this morning."

"Fine time to be finding that out!" Akins grumbled.

Terring continued, unperturbed. "And, if none of the rest of you have developed any symptoms, I might consider lifting the quarantine today."

"You mean it, Doc?"

"We're all right. Please, Doc, let us out of here!"

FRESHMAN QUARTERBACK

"I can't stand this any longer! These guys are driving me nuts!"

Terring ignored their protests. After inspecting tongues, examining neck glands, and taking temperatures, he walked briskly upstairs to Reynolds's room. He found the bored athlete doing sit-ups on the floor. Terring breathed a sigh of relief. What he had hoped for was confirmed. It was a false alarm. Still, it had served its purpose.

He delivered the good news and was nearly knocked down by the rush as the stars headed for wide-open spaces. Terring followed, relieved that his plan had not been necessary. He drove cheerfully back to his office; Terring was always happy when his patients recovered their health. He was especially happy he had not compromised his Hippocratic oath to bring about the desired results.

Fireball Finley spent the rest of the morning at the business office. He smiled as he tucked the Jeff dorm receipt into his backpack. Right after lunch, he lugged two big suitcases down the steps to a waiting taxi. Fireball had already said good-bye to the few housemates he respected. Pete Pines, Bebop Leopoulos, Lonnie Akins, and Sean Reynolds watched with bitter malice in their eyes but not enough courage in their hearts to challenge their former friend as he left.

After Jefferson Hall's Pete Randolph got Fireball settled on the third floor, Finley headed for B. G. Anderson's office. He waited patiently for two hours in the reception room. Fireball's thoughts shifted to freshman practice and Nik Nelson. Football had been the most important thing in Fireball's life, and he had made a hard decision.

Out on Alumni Field, a zealous young coach was being himself for the first time since the start of practice at Camp Sundown. Coach Nik Nelson was happy with himself and had regained his self-respect. He had responded to the enthusiastic efforts of the Jeff team as he had as a youngster to the call of baseball in the spring. When the subdued Booster stars showed up, Nelson took it in stride, showing no emotion. It was up to them to prove themselves now. He had his team. But he did miss Fireball Finley.

About that time, Biz Anderson was welcoming Fireball into his office. "It's good to see you. I'm sure glad Dr. Terring lifted the quarantine. We need you guys real bad for A. & M."

"I—"

"Now don't worry about anything! We'll just forget the letter and everything else that happened. You can pick up that SUV whenever you want and as far as a job and moving out of the Booster house are concerned—"

"I've already moved, Mr. Anderson."

"You what?"

"I've moved into Jeff, and I'm looking for a job."

"You mean you're going to quit football? Give up your Booster scholarship?"

Anderson gazed at Finley incredulously, utterly bewildered. What was wrong with this big, good-looking kid? What was wrong with all these youngsters today? First Eddie and now this one. What had gotten into them?

"Why, Fireball, why? *Why* are you doing this crazy thing?"

Anderson sank back weakly in his chair, bewildered and dismayed. That was all the opening Fireball needed.

His words rushed out in a rush, earnest and sincere. "Because I want to be like other students and be a part of what goes on in college. I want to know people for who they are inside and have them know me that way. I want them to know me as a student and as someone who thinks about the future and about something else besides plays and formations and touchdowns.

"I want to be a guy like Chip Hilton—big enough to stand on my own two feet and act responsibly without selling out and acting like a spoiled child. And I want to be respected the way he is!"

B. G. Anderson lost something then, something that left him with a rush. One second it was there; the next it was gone.

He sat quietly at his desk long after Fireball had closed the door softly behind him. He sat there, for the first time questioning the way he was living his own life and the values he was imparting to others. And over and over he kept saying to himself, "He and Eddie said the same thing. Almost the same identical words."

That evening Fireball stood outside Grayson's, looking in. What he saw gave him the confidence to push open the doors and walk inside. Chip was alone behind the counter. Finley glanced sideways at Mitzi and eased himself up on a stool in front of Chip.

"Hi ya, Fireball. It's good to see you. How are you feeling?"

Finley studied Chip's friendly face for a second and then grinned. "Not bad for a guy that's been dodging needles every time he turns his back."

Chip could tell Finley had something else on his mind. "What's going on, Fireball?" he asked.

"A lot of things! Most of all, I need someone to help me get a job. I've moved out of the Booster house and—this'll kill you—into Jeff!"

"No! Really?"

"Yes! Guess this sounds pretty silly, but I'd like to ask for your help in getting a job and learning how to work and how to study."

"Is that all?" Chip smiled and eased Fireball's spirit. "Man, I thought it was something serious. As far as that job, there's an opening right here." Chip gestured toward the cashier's desk. "Of course, if Miss Savrill turns out to be a disturbing influence—"

Finley grinned wryly. "She's disturbing, all right, Chip. But you know something? A big strong guy like me will just have to learn to handle it!"

"OK, come on! We'll see Mr. Grayson. He's back in the office."

"Not so fast! What do I say?"

"Say what's in your heart. Come on!"

Finley got the job and followed Chip back to the front, subdued and thoughtful. "Thanks, Chip," he said sincerely. "Thanks a lot."

"You're welcome, Fireball. See you in the morning."

"You'll see me later if you don't mind, Chip. OK if I wait for you?"

When Chip finished at eleven o'clock, Finley was waiting, and the two friends walked to Jeff. Fireball had wanted to talk to someone about his problems for a long time, and he found that the words came easily when he started.

"I haven't felt right here, Chip. Something's wrong. It isn't at all the way I thought college would be. I thought everyone would be proud of the football team and all of us who played. But I hardly know anybody on campus!"

"Jeff's different. You'll like it there. It's just like a second home. Wait and see."

"You think I'll do OK on that job?" Fireball asked, looking worried. "I've never had a real job before."

"You'll be all right. What about football?"

"I don't know. I guess Nelson's pretty much down on me, and I can't blame him. I'd better drop out for the rest of this year."

"That's foolish. All you have to do is show up and get into your uniform. And you know it!"

"Maybe so, but that isn't the way I want to do it. I want to have a *real* talk with him and clear up some things. I'd like to make a new start."

"He'll be glad to talk to you. Especially with A. & M. coming up. They're undefeated! Look, Fireball, he needs you!"

Finley shook his head. "Me! You're crazy!"

"Oh, no! The Aggies are loaded with subs for every game. They'll to try wear us down. You and I can switch on and off at quarter—"

Finley shook his head vigorously. "Not me, my friend! I'm not going to give anyone a chance to compare me with you. No way. I'm a fullback or a halfback! Look, Chip, I played quarterback in high school because it gave me a chance to run the whole show. But you're the Houdini at that spot. I'm a runner and that's it!"

"Think again," Chip interrupted. "You're the fastest hard-running back I've ever seen!"

Fireball laughed shortly and playfully jabbed Chip in the ribs. "Oh, sure!" he said quickly. "Anyway, a quarterback's got to be able to pass a ball through the eye of a needle. I couldn't hit Biggie Cohen at twenty feet. And as far as my kicking is concerned, forget it!"

"There's lots of other positions. You'd be really good at full or half—"

"I know I can block, and I can back up a line all right, but how do you know Nelson wants any of us?"

"He wants to win that game more than anything in the world. We all do. How 'bout it?"

Finley thought it over. "Maybe I will," he said abruptly. "I'll see him tomorrow. On second thought, I guess I'd better see him tonight. Man, I hope he hasn't gone to bed." He grinned mischievously. "I'm a working man now, you know. Think I'll see him right now! So long!"

Chip stood on Jeff's broad porch and watched the resilient athlete jog easily along the street toward Nelson's apartment. This had been quite an experience. Totally different from anything he had expected. How could a guy change so quickly? Or *had* Fireball Finley changed? Maybe Biggie and Speed and Red and Soapy and Eddie Anderson and Chip Hilton had been wrong all along about the flashy star.

Nik Nelson got a lot of satisfaction out of practice that week. Fireball Finley proved to be the kind of player Nelson always thought he could be. He practiced hard, said nothing, and showed his resourcefulness when he was shifted from one position to another.

Nelson kept Jeff intact most of the time and humiliated the recalcitrant stars by forcing them to learn the dorm plays. But Nik wasn't letting his feelings blind him to the seriousness of the A. & M. game. A victory over these ancient rivals would mean a successful season. So he experimented with what he considered his strongest lineup, never running the players as a team but making sure that each athlete he shifted got a thorough indoctrination.

The annual meeting of the Booster Association was held the day before the big Thanksgiving game. This year, the Boosters were in for a series of surprises. The first was the unexpected attendance of Frank Kinsmore, president of State's Board of Trustees; James Babcock, president of the university; and Walter Murray, dean. By the time they reached coffee and dessert, the Boosters had recovered from that round. Then they ran into a couple of bruising combinations. The first was a knockdown, and the second was a knockout! The president of the association started the fireworks right after he called the meeting to order by announcing his resignation.

"Ladies and gentlemen," Anderson began, "I wish to announce my resignation as president of the association and humbly request your permission to withdraw from membership.

"I am quite sure that most of you are aware of the great enthusiasm I have held for our freshman pilot project. No one was as excited about this opportunity. I urged you to get behind me and follow my lead. But I got off track and misled you. I lost sight of the real purpose of the program State University volunteered to join.

"It disappoints me to say that, although well intentioned, my priorities were out of line. Right from the start, I have been influenced in making this decision by my own son, by one of the outstanding players we recruited, Fireball Finley, and indirectly by Chip Hilton.

"Hilton led his dormitory team to the championship of the league and played a fine game in the annual contest against the freshman. Last Saturday, he led his team to a stirring upset over Oxford while the freshman regulars were under quarantine.

"We can learn a lot from youngsters. Provided we're big enough to do a little listening and take the time to sit down and try to see things from their point of view. Frankly, I was too stubborn to listen to my son. But his firm stance, based on his principles, has taught me there's far more we must do as parents, and more we must do as Boosters, than simply provide financial support.

"Then there was Fireball Finley. Finley is a great football player. I pampered him just as some of the rest of you pamper certain other players we attracted to State. Finley opened my eyes just this week when he withdrew from the Booster house and explained to me how we were doing a disservice and hindering athletes with our overindulgence. They want to stand on their own two feet, and our actions, no matter how well intentioned, prevented them from doing just that.

"That statement probably astonishes you as much as it did me. But Finley was right. We tried to buy their skills and stole their joy of playing football for the love of the game in the process. We set them apart and expected them to maintain the same enthusiasm as the regular student body. We placed them under our outside supervision just like the freshman coaching staff. We disassociated them from normal student life just as we disassociated our coaches from the regular administration of the university.

"Behind my enlightened education is an athlete with whom I have just become acquainted through the eyes of my son. Indeed, at one time, I was under the impression that Chip Hilton was a bad influence on Eddie. I was all wrong. He was a far better influence than I was.

"So, ladies and gentlemen, I'm going to try a little different tactic in my efforts to help State become one of the great educational and athletic institutions of this country. I believe Dr. Kinsmore has a letter outlining my new project, and he may share it with you later in the meeting. Now, if you will excuse me, I've got to hurry home to make sure the house is ready for the Jeff football team dinner this evening."

B. G. Anderson was then shocked by the audience's standing ovation. Biz wasn't present to hear

Dr. Kinsmore's eloquent tribute when the trustee president revealed B. G. Anderson's gift of one million dollars toward the university athletic scholarship fund.

That was just before Kinsmore outlined State University's new freshman athletic policy, which placed all athletic programs, including athletic scholarships, directly under university control and free from any outside interventions.

B. G. Anderson's heart swelled with happiness that night when he saw his son laughing and talking and enjoying the friendship and companionship of a bunch of college freshmen who were as representative of the student body of State University as backpacks, bikes, jeans, and T-shirts are on any college campus.

Biz Anderson got a big kick out of that dinner. Almost as big as Soapy Smith did when Eddie said, "We're all going down to Valley Falls tomorrow, Dad. I'm going to spend the holidays with Chip. His mom has asked all of us down for Thanksgiving dinner, and we're leaving right after the game, if that's OK."

"Driving?"

"Yes, sir."

"Need a car?"

Speed Morris cleared his throat. "No, sir!" he interrupted proudly. Biggie's brother, Abe, is picking up some of the guys, and I'm having *my* car brought up."

Soapy suddenly choked convulsively and covered his face with his napkin. That sounded bad! Biggie thumped him on the back. Soapy recovered for a second, but another glance at Speed's smug expression sent him into hysterics, and he had to leave the table. Everyone began to laugh. Everyone but Speed Morris. Speed failed to appreciate the humor.

CHAPTER 20

From the Heart

FIREBALL FINLEY was experiencing a new sensation, and he didn't like it. Sitting out on an open field during a snowstorm in late November was no joke even if he did have a full-length, heavy warm-up suit thrown over his shoulders and was leaning up against a teammate to shield himself from the icy gusts.

The playing field was a skating rink, and Maxim, McGuire, Rentler, Roberts, Dean, Garcia, Leopoulos, and Gilmore were sitting on the bench, peering through the swirling snow at the action on the field. They didn't like it either. But they didn't say anything. They just fidgeted and turned and watched Coach Nik Nelson like a hawk, trying vainly to catch his eye whenever he turned his head in their direction. A few of the Wonder Team were missing: Sean Reynolds and Pete Pines and Lonnie Akins. They didn't seem to be on the bench. They weren't on the field either. In fact, they weren't even in University. The trio had checked out. They left State early that morning, headed for other opportunities.

Nik Nelson swung his arms and tried to keep warm by walking up and down in front of the bench. Out on the field Jeff's fighting dorm champs presented a curious sight. All wore long cleats, and everyone except Chip wore gloves. Soapy was different. He turned up with a pair of bright red gloves on his hands and ear muffs inside his helmet. Most of the time the ear muffs skewed out from under his headgear and over his eyes, but Soapy didn't mind. He was frozen stiff.

It was tough to get a start, tough to dig in on the icy turf. Going into the fourth quarter, the game was scoreless, a standoff filled with very uninteresting football. Chip and his A. & M. passing opponent found out early in the game that going up top was out of the question, and the game developed into a rushing and kicking contest.

The Thanksgiving Day crowd had frozen up right after the opening kickoff, and the spectators were literally sitting on their hands. There wasn't much to cheer about, and there wasn't much protection from the storm in Alumni Field's stands. But the State fans weren't going to walk out on this game. Pride and tradition were important elements in any contest with A. & M. A victory over an Aggie team signified a successful season for any State squad, even if it was the only win of the year.

Chip was worn out, and he had plenty of company. Joel Ohlsen, Tug Rankin, and Bull Warner could barely stand. They weren't asking for mercy, but it was written in the tired lines in their faces and in the glazed expressions in their eyes. The A. & M. coach had taken advantage of his superior numbers and was subbing his players in and out.

Joel, Tug, and Bull weren't going to ask to be taken out, and Chip Hilton sure wasn't about to suggest it. Not after coaxing them to come out in the first place and then stay out to win the dorm championship. No, they were going right down to the wire together.

The A. & M. rushers finally located a weak spot and ran over Joel's tackle position and through Tug and Bull on every kick. Chip had barely gotten the last desperate punt away. Now he was backed up to his goal line and had to kick again.

He gave the count and the green shirts seemed to come with the ball, swarming toward him in a solid wave. He kicked away and, with a heart that froze in his body, heard the dull thud as the ball met someone's chest and went bounding up and back over his head. Chip forced his tired legs to spin his body around and carry him after the skittering pigskin.

Ten feet away, he dove along the icy ground, and his frozen fingers closed on the ball just as the A. & M. rushers crashed over him. The ball slid out of his hands and across the goal line. Momentum carried him along, and he regained control just as the whole A. & M. team piled on him, wrenching and tearing at his arms, trying to wrest the ball away, to steal it under the blanket of bodies. Chip fought to hold on, but he was sick at heart. He knew it was a safety. Two points in this kind of game were as good as twenty.

Chip was right; a cheer went up from the visitors when the referee signaled the score.

The clock showed seven minutes to go when he elected to punt from the twenty-yard line after the safety. The ball carried to the A. & M. forty and ended up at midfield when the sure-handed Aggie receiver took a chance on the catch and brought it back. Chip called his second time-out of the half and evaluated the situation.

Nik Nelson shared Chip's concern, but there was

something more involved here than a victory. He looked at the clock. Six minutes to go, behind 2-0 in the score.

Fireball shifted his feet and bunched his muscles. If Nelson would only give him a chance! What was wrong with him? Couldn't he see Chip and the rest of the Jeffs were worn out?

A. & M.'s weight began to tell. The Aggies' skillful quarterback held the ball, smashed away at Ohlsen's spot, and drove steadily down to the twenty, where Chip, in desperation, took his third and final time-out.

Fireball couldn't stand it any longer. He broke just when Nelson had figured he would and leaped from the bench. "Look, Coach," Fireball pleaded, "give us a chance! They're all used up! Come on! We've learned our lesson."

Coach Nelson deliberated, looking from one star to another. "I believe you have," he said thoughtfully. "I believe you have. All right, Finley! In for Warner! Maxim for Ohlsen! McGuire-Rankin! Garcia-Schwartz! Gilmore-Waldorf! Leopoulos-English! On the double!"

No matter how tired a player is, he never wants to come out of a football game. Chip breathed a sigh of thankfulness. Guys get hurt when they're tired. Nelson had struck it just right and chosen the players who most needed a rest. Chip sized up Biggie, Speed, and Soapy and grinned when he caught their knowing smiles. No one could knock those three out of the game!

"We've got to hold 'em, guys," he said in the huddle. "They won't take a chance on a pass, so we'll use our 6-3-2 defense. Speed, you play back with me. Come on now, dig in!"

And they did! Fireball, Bebop, and Mike were in on every play, ferociously backing up the line. Their fight and spirit spread to the front line, and the Aggies couldn't gain an inch. On fourth down A. & M. went into place-kick formation. The kicker made too much of a show about the spot where the quarterback should place the ball and calculated the angle until his teammates warned him about the time.

Chip called for a 6-2-2-1 defense and backed up in the end zone in front of the goal posts. Right then, familiar little warning signals began hammering away in the back of his head. The kicker had put on *too much* of an act. It was almost unbelievable that the A. & M. quarterback would take such a silly chance. Was he going to pass? Where? To whom?

Chip glanced at the clock. Two minutes and twenty seconds. It had to be now or never. He remembered Rock always saying a team might as well lose by nine points as two. *Where would he throw in this situation? He wouldn't!* But A. & M. was going to! Would the Aggies pass in Speed's or in McGuire's territory? They would try out the newcomer, of course! They'd pass to their left!

"69-47-38-23—"

Chip started to his right on the snap of the ball, leaving his territory wide open. It was bad football, but he was playing a hunch. He'd tried to pass earlier and knew how hard it was just to hold the slippery ball much less fake with it. No, it would be a timed pass. The ball sped to the quarterback, and the kicker ran forward and followed through with the kick. But there wasn't a thud! Out to Chip's right, A. & M.'s left end had drawn McGuire clear to the sideline, a perfect decoy.

Timing it perfectly, the Aggie left halfback delayed long enough for the area to clear and then cut for the ball, which was already wobbling through the air into McGuire's vacated zone.

Chip arrived first, leaped high in the air, came down with the ball, and nearly fell flat on his face. Clawing desperately, he managed to keep his feet and hold the ball. Then he headed upfield. The stunned receiver pivoted and gave chase. Chip's long strides drew him steadily away, but the kicker and quarterback were angling ahead, racing for the right sideline far down the field, certain to intercept him unless he got help. Unfortunately, no help was possible. Chip's teammates had been tricked by the fake kick and were left far behind.

The fans in Alumni Field were on their feet now, yelling hysterically. It was the first real action of the game, and their frozen discomfort was forgotten. Chip flashed past the forty, the forty-five, midfield, the forty-five, and the forty. The Aggie kicker made his try right there, missing the tackle, but slowing Chip down enough to allow the quarterback to knock him out of bounds. Chip had tried to change direction, but it was impossible; his cleats just wouldn't hold.

So, there State was, first down and ten on the Aggie thirty-yard line, behind 2-0 with fifty seconds to play. The out-of-bounds tackle had helped by stopping the clock. Chip's mind was racing. He hadn't clicked with a pass all morning, and it was too far for a placement. He *had* to throw the ball. At least, an incomplete pass would stop the clock.

In the huddle, Chip hurried his instructions. He couldn't afford a penalty for taking too much time now. "Heads up, guys! We've *got* to pass! It's the only way we can save time. If a pass clicks, make the catch, then get out of bounds. Another thing. No huddle! Got it? No huddle! We'll try nothing but short passes! OK? Hang on if you get it! Fifty-five on three! Let's go!"

"55-62-43—"

Chip faked to Speed and Fireball, pivoted, and tried his jump pass. It clicked! Soapy went up in the middle of a scramble of arms and bodies and somehow came down with the ball on the twenty-eight-yard line. But the play had used up twenty precious seconds.

There were fifteen seconds to go when Chip tried his basketball toss again. He passed to Garcia this time, but Hector leaped too soon and batted the ball in the air. Half a dozen Aggies made frenzied attempts to grasp the slippery ball, but it eluded their cold-stiffened fingers and fell to the ground, incomplete, again stopping the clock!

Two seconds to go! Time for one play!

Chip's teammates hurried to the line of scrimmage, holding their breath, fear in their eyes, despair in their hearts.

Chip gauged the distance and the angle and hesitated. Twenty-eight yards to the goal line . . . ten more to the crossbar, plus the height . . . and snow and ice on the ground!

Finley made the decision. Confidently and aggressively. "You can do it, Chip! Come on! Kick it over the grandstand!"

That was it! Chip showed Speed where to place the snap and then dropped back two long steps. He didn't look up, but he heard Fireball say, "No one's getting through this line, Chip. Take your time."

"44-69-57—"

Speed plunked the ball down, and Chip gave it all he had, meeting the ball with all the power that desperation, hope, and prayer can give.

Chip didn't look up. He never saw the referee's arms shoot above his head. But he heard the roar from the stands and the joyous cheers of his teammates. And he was still looking down at the scuff-marked snow, trying to spit the cotton out of his mouth, when Fireball gathered him in his powerful arms and hoisted him up on

Biggie's shoulders. They were all around him then, shouting and punching and shoving him higher and higher until he felt as though he were riding a giant breaker.

"You did it, Chip! You did it!"

Chip tried to fight his way down through the forest of high fives, pats on the helmet, and slaps on the back, but he didn't have a chance. He had to take it, take the bouncing and the pounding and the cheering all the way to the bench. There he scrambled down to receive Coach Nelson's firm handshake and some whacks on the back. Then it started all over again. The guys on the bench wanted to show him how they felt, so up he went again. And that's where he stayed, all the way to the locker room under the stands.

That didn't end it either! Someone turned on a shower, and in he went, uniform and all! At least it was warm! He finally fought his way out to be peppered with socks, jerseys, shoulder pads, and anything else they could find. Chip loved it. Who wouldn't? It was from the heart!

Soapy Smith had been yelling for five minutes and finally made his voice heard. It was time to go to Valley Falls! It was Thanksgiving, and Soapy knew how his mom and Mary Hilton could cook.

"C'mon, you guys! C'mon, I'm starvin'! Let's get out of here! Turkey, here we come!"

That did it! Ten minutes later, they were dressed and on their way, followed by a chorus of advice and good-natured insults. Speed led them through a maze of cars to the red Mustang fastback parked right at the gate and raring to go.

Finley feigned alarm. "Five of us in that?" he cried. "It can't be done!"

"That's what you think!" Soapy bellowed, diving for the front seat.

"Nothing to it!" Biggie shouted. "Go on! You'll get used to it, Fireball. Red and Petey are coming with Abe and me."

"It's only a couple of hours!" Schwartz barked. "Step on it!"

Eddie Anderson circled around Fireball and made the back seat in one leap. "I'm ready," he shouted. "Let her roll!"

Speed Morris slid in behind the wheel, and the sports car groaned as they scrambled and fought for seats. While they were still floundering around for seat space, Speed stepped on the gas, and they were on their way.

"Gimme *some* room!" Eddie complained, elbowing Cohen in the ribs.

"Quit shovin'!" Fireball retorted. "I *can't* move!"

"Ouch! Get off!" Chip yelled.

"Bet you guys could make room for *Mitzi!*" Speed roared.

There was a loud "Bah!" from Soapy. "Women!" he snorted.

Chip grinned and glanced sideways at Finley. Fireball grinned widely too. "And how!" he bellowed.

Eddie Anderson reached forward and gleefully batted Soapy over the head. Surprisingly, Soapy didn't say a word. He just hunched down until only his flaming hair and two equally red ears could be seen.

The Hilton A. C. would have a few new members for Thanksgiving. And new friends in the Hilton home too!

• • •

FRESHMAN QUARTERBACK

You won't want to miss the exciting
story of how Chip makes the freshman
basketball team. Make a fast break for your
nearest bookstore to get your copy of
Backboard Fever.

Afterword

WE ARE about to enter a new millennium. This is a time not only to anticipate the future, but also to examine our values and to determine how we are going to face the challenges of the twenty-first century. The importance of perseverance, teamwork, integrity, and fairness are as important to America's success in the next one hundred years as they were in the twentieth century.

Those involved with intercollegiate sports are committed to fostering an environment that is supportive of fair play and respectful of all competitors. Integrity, fair play, and ethical behavior are not just words, but rather constitute the elements of noble sports behavior. It is the responsibility of sport coaches at all levels to see that these standards are encouraged. For this reason I am pleased to see the reissuance of the Chip Hilton series.

The Chip Hilton books and the fictional character of Chip Hilton provide fine examples of the importance of integrity and determination as well as physical prowess, not only on the playing field but also in one's everyday life. We are constantly faced with challenges; how we face and overcome these challenges determines what kind of person we are.

We hear the words *role model* quite often connected to sports figures. These books, in an important way, portray a sports figure whose demonstrated integrity and determination speak with power in today's world. The concepts of integrity and good sportsmanship are not old-fashioned, but rather are at the foundation of the American sports concept. We, as sports administrators and as parents, are responsible for directing our children to reach their highest potential in an honest and ethical manner.

The Chip Hilton series of books provide great reading and important lessons for all who love great stories about the value and values of sports.

JIM DELANY
Commissioner, Big Ten Conference

Your Score Card

I have I expect to
read: to read:

_____ _____ 1. *Touchdown Pass:* The first story in the series, which introduces you to William "Chip" Hilton and all his friends at Valley Falls High during an exciting football season.

_____ _____ 2. *Championship Ball:* With a broken ankle and an unquenchable spirit, Chip wins the state basketball championship and an even greater victory over himself.

_____ _____ 3. *Strike Three!* In the hour of his team's greatest need, Chip Hilton takes to the mound and puts the Big Reds in line for all-state honors.

____ ____ 4. ***Clutch Hitter!*** Chip's summer job at the Mansfield Steel Company gives him a chance to play baseball on the famous Steeler team where he uses his head as well as his war club.

____ ____ 5. ***A Pass and a Prayer:*** Chip's last football season is a real challenge as conditions for the Big Reds deteriorate and somehow he must keep the team together for their coach.

____ ____ 6. ***Hoop Crazy:*** When three-point fever spreads to the Valley Falls basketball varsity, Chip Hilton has to do something, and do it fast!

____ ____ 7. ***Pitchers' Duel:*** Valley Falls participates in the state baseball tournament, and Chip Hilton pitches in a nineteen-inning struggle fans will long remember. The Big Reds year-end banquet isn't to be missed!

____ ____ 8. ***Dugout Jinx:*** Chip's graduated and has one more high school game before beginning a summer internship with a minor league team during its battle for the league pennant.

____ ____ 9. ***Freshman Quarterback:*** Early autumn finds Chip Hilton and four of his Valley Falls friends at Camp Sundown, the temporary site of State University's freshman and varsity football teams. Join them in Jefferson Hall to share the successes, disappointments, and pranks as they begin their freshman year.

*Visit your local bookstore
or contact Broadman & Holman Publishers
for all these books!*

more great releases from the

Chip Hilton ★ Sports Series

by Coach Clair Bee

The sports-loving boy, born out of the imagination of Clair Bee, is back! Clair Bee first began writing the Chip Hilton series in 1948. During the next twenty years, over two million copies of the series were sold. Written in the tradition of the *Hardy Boys* mysteries, each book in this 23-volume series is a positive-themed tale of human relationships, good sportsmanship, and positive influences–things especially crucial to young boys in the '90s. Through these larger-than-life fictional characters, countless young people have been exposed to stories that helped shape their lives.

WELCOME BACK, CHIP HILTON!

Vol. 1 - Touchdown Pass
0-8054-1686-2

Vol. 2 - Championship Ball
0-8054-1815-6
Vol. 3 - Strike Three!
0-8054-1816-4
Vol. 4 - Clutch Hitter!
0-8054-1817-2
Vol. 5 - A Pass and a Prayer
0-8054-1987-X
Vol. 6 - Hoop Crazy
0-8054-1988-8
Vol. 7 - Pitchers Duel
0-8054-1989-6
Vol. 8 - Dugout Jinx
0-8054-1990-X
Vol. 9 - Freshman Quarterback
0-8054-1991-8
Vol. 10 - Backboard Fever
0-8054-1992-6

available at fine bookstores everywhere